ELYSIUM

Michael Edgerly

Order this book online at www.trafford.com
or email orders@trafford.com

Most Trafford titles are also available at major online book retailers.

Printed in the United States of America.

ISBN: 978-1-4269-0016-7 (sc)

ISBN: 978-1-4269-0017-4 (hc)

ISBN: 978-1-4269-0018-1 (e-book)

*Our mission is to efficiently provide the world's finest, most comprehensive book publishing
service, enabling every author to experience success. To find out how to publish your book,
your way, and have it available worldwide, visit us online at www.trafford.com*

Trafford rev. 7/21/2010

 www.trafford.com

North America & international
toll-free: 1 888 232 4444 (USA & Canada)
phone: 250 383 6864 ♦ fax: 812 355 4082

PROLOGUE

The day everyone died at the field marked the last for Timothy Peters. The day could have gone without incident but the wind was just right and he new it was time to rid of the burden. Most of the day's work had been done and the majority of the slaves had returned to their quarters for supper. They understood the master wasn't a right man and that his mind was leaving. He had never hurt anyone and in recent years had given freedom to more than half of them. Only fifty seven were left and they were treated quite well. The foremen were nice and although times were sometimes hard, they had realized that most other plantations couldn't share equal comments. That afternoon was entirely different. Master Peters had come back from being away and when he walked into the quarters he had this stare. He never said a word he just stood at the door and looked upon them. The children played in the back of the room and most of the elders tried to hush them down as Peters started to stroll towards the back. They were surprised at his presence and some even whispered the assumption because he never had come to the quarters at this hour. "The fields have called to me." He spoke loudly as he walked. "Do you know of the fields?" He looked around the room at the confused faces. The children had now quieted down and the elders held them on their laps. No one answered and Tim turned and walked back towards the door. He paced from one side of the room to the other as they watched and stared. Tim noticed a hook at the far end of the quarters, which hung some rope, and he turned his head as if he heard a noise outside. He walked to the door and swung it open. There at the far end of the yard a tree swayed in the breeze. The sky was growing a deep blue and the tree seemed to reach for what light remained. "What," he called out. The others inside began to talk back and forth and panic began to rise among them. Some of the children could sense the tension and began to cry out. Tim turned and eyeballed the group before him. He walked out and slammed the door behind him. They could hear him outside calling for his foreman. The wind picked up and the sky began to twist with colors as the tree danced back and forth. "You want them?" he yelled into the field. His madness had boiled over and the foreman came to his aide trying to get him inside. He ripped away from them and pointed his fingers swearing for them to leave him and gather the slaves at the tree. They ignored his request and tried to talk him back to the house. Peters lashed out at them with his fists and swore he would have them executed if they didn't do as he commanded. His hair danced in the wind covering most of his contorted face. His maddening smile spread across his face like Cheshire cat as he looked up at the tree and raised his hands, "You, it is you that will take them to my field!" The men went to the quarters and gathered them all, lining them up under the tree, the mothers holding their children to their chests protecting them from the wind. Peters ran to the house and on his way told a few of the hands to gather as much rope as they could find. When he returned to the yard he had a shot gun in his hands. The foreman looked on and stood in front of the group. "String the rope," he yelled at the men, "There on that tree, the fields call boys!" he laughed and his mouth was so wide that it looked like it engulfed his face. While the rope was being hung from the tree Peters looked out to the fields and walked to the yards edge. In the distance he could see little eyes dancing within the grass. His smile faded and he grimaced as he raised his gun. He fired off a couple of shots at the eyes and grunted when they popped up and bobbed back and forth, mocking him. He walked into the field and raised his gun, "Get out of my field!" he yelled. The men turned towards the slaves and tried to calm them. Most of them were frozen in fear as they watched the other hands prepare the ropes. They understood what would happen and they pleaded with the foreman. One of them stepped forward past the men and looked out at the master. The young black man watched the farmer rant and rave back and forth in the field and looked out to see what the master was yelling at. The grass swayed violently as its whispers called to them and one of the men turned him and asked him to please join the others until they could calm the master. Tim turned and he raised his gun shooting the men in the back. As he fell to the ground the young man looked up at Timas he felt were the bullet ripped through his chest. Children screamed and the slaves held their hands up and began to panic. The men just stopped and stared at Tim, the fields and the two dead in the yard. Master Peters turned back to the eyes, "I am the master of these fields." He pointed to them. "No one will have this field!" He shot off a few more rounds ranting at the eyes as they danced. He reloaded and then returned to the yard. The wind blew his hair from his face and he smiled from ear to ear. "I am the master." He laughed. The sky was black and the tree loomed over the yard as it rocked back and forth in fury. The master held up his arms and mimicked its branches as he cackled at the men. "Do you all understand? I am the master!" Tim walked up to the young slave laying dead in his yard. He bent down and looked him in the face, his smile faded. His heart was heavy as he realized what he had done. He showed his teeth and stood up looking right at the men. "See what you have made me do." He yelled and raised his gun. "You leave me no choice!" The day everyone died at the field marked the last for Timothy Peters. The day could have gone without incident but the wind was just right.

CHAPTER 1

The doctor's office is a cold place for most people, the tables with their flimsy paper that made that crinkly sound every time you moved. Nurses that never seems to stay long, probably an intern, and walls, that even if they had color, seemed alone and unforgiving to the patient. The only two things that are of comfort are: youalways see the same doctor and you get to leave. Jody stared at her son and thought of all the times they had spent in the same room. He sat unknowing and played with his star wars figures. It always seemed to be the same battle to her, a man dressed in black and an android of some kind. He would make the laser gun sound and whisper, "AHHH" and the droid would fall. Every so often a silhouette would pass by the frosted crack of glass embedded in the door and Jody would sit up and then hunch when it passed them by, not the doc. Fixing her skirt she crossed her legs in the opposite direction, *and another thing, these chairs suck.* Fishing around in her purse she found some chap stick and took as much time as she could to apply it to pass the time. The list would climb as she complained to herself, *no clocks on the walls, what are they doing, why does the droid always die?*She looked at her son again and relaxed. This was to find out what was going on with him, she needed to remember that. The door swung open and she sat in attention once again. He shut the door quietly behind him and peered up at Jody from the top of his glasses.

1

The doctor walked over to her hand shook her hand, "Mrs. Burns." She gave her usual smile and sat quietly. Doc turned to Tristan, "How's my patient today?" "Droid lost again huh." Tristan smiled and put them down. "Yup, he can't beat the Jedi Mr. Tolbert!" Jody smiled as the doc fixed his glasses and turned toward the counter, placing the chart open. "The seizures seemed to be progressing, is that right Mrs. Burns?" Jody confirmed and looked at Tristan who just looked around the room, oblivious to what they were talking about. "We have several tests to talk about and I would like him to see another specialist, if that's ok with you?" Jody once again shook her head yes and clasped her hands on her knees. "Do you have any idea what is causing this?" Her voice was shaky and the doc looked at her with a lost look. "I understand you're worried and we are doing everything we can to figure out what Tristan's brain is doing." "We are scheduling another doctor at the hospital to take some CAT scans again and see what it is we are missing; I think we will make progress there." Jody rubbed her hands together and held back her emotions. She didn't want to scare Tristan. "Everything else looks great, EKG is normal, Blood work is normal. Has he been sleeping well?" She smiled, "Like an angel." The doc looked at Tristan and patted him on the knee, "How about a sucker?" Tristan sprung up and grabbed his things and followed the doctor out the door to the reception desk. Jody put her head in her lap and put her frustration and fear aside. She trusted doc and he has taken great care of Tristan since he first met them. They reentered the room and doc rubbed Tristan on the head causing him to look up with a wince. "I will see the both of you back next week and in the meantime I will call you with the specialists name, address, date and time, k." The walk to the car was another thing that is a benefit. As soon as you sit down and grip the wheel, it feels as if for a second something new will happen. When you hit your first red light and notice the busy bodies around you is where you become grounded once again. Tristan eyed the McDonald's from at least eight blocks away and it was going to be where lunch was taking place today. The line inside seemed as if everyone in the city was on lunch at the same time. Customers barking out orders as the teenagers ran back and forth, confused and chaotic. "Come on!" a man shouted from somewhere ahead as children cried and business men checked their watches. Tristan was untouched by all of this and stood waiting like a saint. He had his eyes on the prize and if he was lucky, the one Jedi toy he was missing would be waiting for him in the bag. When they finally made it to the counter Jody was about to pass out from hunger and just called out a number off the menu. Tristan ordered the same thing as he always does, chicken kids meal with a chocolate milkshake. Before they could even find a seat he had grabbed his bag off the tray and began shuffling around to find his toy. Pulling it out like the Holy Grail and then giving a sigh when it was a repeater, "I have this one." Jody found a small booth facing the street and quickly set up Tristan's food for him. "So what are we gonna do with this Jedi?" Tristan picked up a nugget and shrugged his shoulders. "I could feed him to the rancor monster." "The what?" Jody smiled. Tristan shook his head in disappointment. "It's a creature that is owned by Jabba the Hut!" "Never mind mom, it's not something you would understand-k." They continued to eat for a few minutes in silence. Jody wouldn't laugh at his seriousness on the subject and if she did he would not speak to her for the rest of the day, until he needed snack or dinner anyway. She stared at him for a bit, watching him eat and create his sound effects, thinking when this would all blow over. *"Never?"* she whispered. "What mommy?" Jody sprang up and smiled. "Let's get out of here we have to get dinner ready, dad will be home soon!" Tristan scooped up his new recruitment and stuffed him in his pocket as he slid out from booth. They shuffled through the crowd, which was now at full throttle. "Stay with me Tristan." Nodding his head, he rolled his eyes "Yup." She pointed her keychain and as she heard the click to unlock the door Tristan stood stiff as stone. She caught it out the corner of her eye and spun to his attention, "Tristan honey?" His eyes glazed over and he pointed to his ear. "Do you hear them mommy?" "They need to know you hear them." Jody knelt before him and put her hands out a little. The doctor had told her never to touch him during this state. Most patients could go into hysteria and they may attack. "Listen mommy, they told me you never listen." Tristan reached in his pocket and felt around a bit. "Tristan, relax baby. Mommy's here." Retrieving a quarter he held it straight out to his left. He began to look around as if responding to noise or some type of command. "They need to be satisfied they are heard, when will you listen to them?" Tristan's voice became harsh and demanding. "Tristan honey, this is mommy. I don't understand baby. Who needs to be heard?" This was the routine. He always said the same thing over and over. Seldom he would look her in the eye and tell her they are coming for him because *you* can't listen. Jody tried to find out and understand who *they* were. Tristan never said a name and this day was no different. He looked her in the eye and then turned his head a little staring at her ear. "No you don't. You won't listen and I have told you every time mommy. Stop worrying about the boy Jody and listen to us." She sat back looking up at him. This was new. He had never spoken as something or someone else and his eyes were cold and this was *not* Tristan. He opened his hand and dropped the quarter to the ground. Jody watched as He collapsed precisely as the quarter touched the cement. She grabbed her son as he lay on the ground while people watched with confusion. "Somebody call an ambulance, and stop staring!" People just stood, confused and trying to believe what they had just witnessed. "Please," she screamed. "Stop staring and help." She rocked her boy and breathed deeply as she heard the sound of a distant ambulance. He would be okay. This has happened many times before and like many other times, he would look up at her in the hospital bed and the coldness would be gone. Strong like his father was what her mother said from the day she laid eyes on him. Jody was thinking that this was a good time to think about other things and let the doctors do their job. When she worried, false assumptions seemed to find a way into her head. Doctors had lectured her many times on staying positive and letting them get solid answers before jumping into deep water. The waiting room looked like all others, white on white, symbolizing clean. That smell that always lingered in the room told another story. Strangers who were there for the same reason, waiting. She felt relieved that Tristan never stayed behind those doors for very long and she could take him home and coddle him until they both felt safe, until she felt safe anyway. *Who could feel safe here?* No clocks and no calendars. Just people sitting in cubicles, every so often looking up to see if you need something. "Mrs. Burns", it always seemed to be the same voice, like news reporters. "Partly cloudy with a chance of rain", it could be a man or a woman and it would make no difference. Jody turned and stood up facing a young man who seemed to be maybe twenty-five years old. "Hello Mrs. Burns, could you follow me down to your son's room please." She gathered her things and had to walk quickly not to lose him around the corner. "Is Tristan ok?" The doctor turned his head as he looked at his clip board. "He is sleeping still and we need to ask you some questions before you see him, ok?" She was confused. It had always been the same. They would come and get her, she would ask if he was ok and they would lead her down a corridor to his room where she would find him either sleeping or sitting up playing with his toys. "What type of questions, Mr.?" He stopped suddenly and turned toward her. "Excuse me", he smiled "I am Doctor Martin." extending his right hand. "Standard questions really Mrs. Burns, just want to know some family history, episode frequency, personal behaviors." She was sure he was leaving something out. "I'm sure that his records at his specialist could answer those for you." He didn't respond and with a swift turn of a corner, led her into an office room with a conference table in the middle. She felt like she was part of one of those weird FBI shows were they are yelling back and forth at their captive until he gives away the plot. "Please sit," he smiled. "The rest of the doctors will be here shortly." She walked to a seat and heard the door shut behind her. Setting down her coat and purse she quickly went to the door and opened it to the hallway. The young doctor had gone and the halls were empty and quite. Jody stood for a few minutes and looked back and forth down the hallways in search of some kind of life, *where is my boy?* The brown leather seats were cold and they gave a woe as she sat down slowly and folded her hands on her legs. The table was oak with a deep red stain, very expensive. It was clean and empty except for a conference phone placed as perfect to the middle as humanly possible. It looked as though it had never been touched though she was sure it had plenty of conference hours clocked in. The walls were white as every room in the hospital and not one picture or painting, calendar or clock was on the walls. *I hate hospitals.* She could hear some voices coming around the corner and before she could decipher the destination, two men walked into the room and slammed some folders on the table. Jody watched as they acted oblivious to her attendance. They bickered about who was picking up the bar tab the coming weekend and only noticed her when three very well dressed suits came into the room and sat at the table facing Jody. "Hello Mrs. Burns, we just have a few questions to ask you and then these two doctors have a few as well, ok." Jody just sat there and shook her head confused and worried. The suits sat down and slapped a folder on the desk in front of them. Eye contact was sparing and Jody was beginning to sense there was more to this than "we have a few questions." The two doctors sat quietly and looked through there folders. The suit on the left looked up and took a deep breath and looked her dead in the eyes. "My name is Officer Mitchelle these are my associates, Officer Kent and officer Brunnel." "Your son", looking at his file, "Tristan?" Jody nodded when he peered up at her, "He has said some things that a nurse has taken alarm to. We had been called in and were witnessed to some of these allegations and need some history about Tristan as well as you and your husband". The house was dark and cold when Dustin strolled in at six. He usually smelled dinner and was greeted by "hello honey!" while Tristan grappled to his hip. This could be one of those nights that she visited her mother and with that thought he was glad to be missing out. He stood in the door way for a minute and shuffled in his coat for his cell phone. The light made him look hideous in the dark as he found Jody's cell number. He shook off his coat and hung it on an empty chair as he swung the door shut and walked towards the kitchen. The phone crackled a bit, country living, and her voice greeted him and promptly asked to leave a message. It fooled him every time and he would almost respond, smile then wait for the beep. "Honey, just making sure everything is alright. I will get dinner started. Let me know that you're ok please. Love you." Dustin turned the lights and sighed at the emptiness and stretched his back a bit. A pile of dishes greeted him in the sink and he promptly turned down the offer. As he rummaged through the cupboards to find something edible he shifted his thoughts a little towards the big meeting next week. The systems manager at the lab harped on Dustin to make a new budget plan for next year. As long as he had been a consulting exec he focused only on their business. It didn't turn into "come to see my kids and the wife in Florida", Bahamas, whatever. He knew people that took the perk and it sank them every time. At most, they would last four to six years until the firm tired of paying perk trips to clients and replaced him or her with a newbie. He always just politely turned offers down and smiled on his way to his office. Hence he had been there fifteen years and had kept the same clients with very little change. The only perks he indulged in were the free meals and the yearly company picnic that was really a Vegas trip to the casinos to lose what they had made the year before. "Mac and cheese, Sloppy Joes?" he shut the doors and stared at the fridge for a minute. "Jody would have had something whipped up, ahh." He loved the fact that she could be home to care for Tristan, it made dinner easier for sure. He hated that she had given up her career. He made more money and that was her justification, but he felt she was neglected. He had offered many times in the past to switch roles for a year or two. He could work out of the home and she could get out and get what she loved back, her business. She insisted that she would feel guilty leaving Tristan home and that he needed her. He would just let her have her way but knew that one day it would haunt him, like taking perks. His cell rang out, startling him. "Hello." Jody's soft voice eased him as she confirmed her arrival within the next fifteen minutes. "At your mother's?" he chuckled. She didn't laugh back and said she would talk to him when they got home and Tristan went to bed. Dustin looked around in the dark puzzled and let it go. "Alright honey, I'm trying to find something for dinner." "I ordered pizza." she answered back. He smiled and realized she was aware of what he was doing and saved them all from what might have transpired. "It should be there soon and we will see you when we get there. Tristan is very tired. He had another episode today. Like I said we will talk later." "Is he okay?" Jody was quite for what seemed forever. "Yeah, he is just tired that's all, love you." Dustin closed his phone and walked over to the table and sat down. He looked around the room and took a deep breath while he thought about what they were going to do for Tristan. He stood up and walked around the house, turning on lights and setting the table. He didn't want them entering the house the way he did. It needed to look lively. Turning on the front porch light, he peered out into the darkness and up the road to see if he could spot their car in the distance. The outside now resembled how the inside of the house looked minutes ago, dark, and alone. When the pizza arrived Dustin shook his head when a teenager delivered it with more metal on his face than the car he owned. It didn't bother him but he just wanted to tell the boy that his career was hard pressed if he continued the trend. He was beginning to sound like his dad. A fifteen dollar pizza turned to twenty when Dustin felt pity and tipped him greatly. The sound of some heavy metal music resonated from his passenger door as he ran back to his car, slammed the door and slid over his hood like Bo and Luke Duke.

Walking back to the kitchen he heard the car speed off into the dark when headlights pierced the front door window. He dropped the pizza on the table and rushed to the door to help Jody with Tristan. As he stepped out to the porch, Tristan grappled his waist, "daddy!" Jody walked up behind Tristan and kissed her husband hard. Tristan let go and threw his hand in the air. "Look at this new Jedi I got at Mickey Dees Dad!" Dustin bent to exam the toy. "Ah, this must be number seven?" Tristan laughed, "I don't know dad, I got so many." "I have so many." Jody smiled as she walked past them and piled her coat on top of Dustin's. Pizza filled the air and she walked over and giggled at the place setting. "It was only pizza honey, we could use paper plates." Dustin walked in with Tristan and they sat at their designated seats. "Well, I thought we were eating fancy tonight." She shook her head as her boys plowed into the box. Watching with amazement as they piled two or three slices at a time on their plate and snatching up a slice before the monsters left her with nothing but a growling stomach. Tristan told his dad about the day and the hospital, the ambulance ride that he could only faintly remember. It was like a journey for him every time, as if going to fun park and these were the rides. Jody tried not to think of it all and let Tristan spin his tale while they shook their heads in amazement as if hearing it once again for the first time. They would sneak questions in about what he felt like when the "episode" started. Did he remember what he had said and what the voice had said? Tristan could recite it verbatim and would only stop in short breaths to remember specifics about the voice. Never once did he show fear and they tried to keep theirs at bay while he told them of his experience. It became quite for a few minutes as they sat back, bellies full. Tristan sat up and looked at his dad very seriously. "I was told that they would be coming soon dad." Dustin sat staring at his boy, "Who?" he asked. "I don't know daddy, I have never seen them. I just hear them." "They said that you guys never listen to them and they need to come and get me so you know." Jody looked at Dustin and got up and walked out into the hallway towards the bathroom. Dustin got up and kneeled before Tristan. "What are we supposed to know Tristan?" "Do they tell you what we are supposed to know?" Tristan shook his head no and shrugged his shoulders. Jody leaned against the wall and held her face in her hands. She began to sob slightly but breathed deep to control it, *Tristan shouldn't hear this.*

Dustin sat back in his chair and smiled at Tristan. "I love you. We will find out what it is and we will make sure you are okay." Tears welled up in his eyes as he looked away. "Don't cry daddy." Tristan got up and climbed on his lap and snuggled in his chest. "They won't hurt me." "They just want mommy and you to listen to what they have to say." Dustin held his boy and Jody sat on the floor in the hallway and began to cry uncontrollably. "Next time daddy I will ask them and they will leave a sign again. Then you can listen." Dustin nodded, "yes, I will listen." When Dustin entered the bedroom and pursed his lips around his finger, Jody knew Tristan had finally had fallen asleep. It took only a few songs, a book or two and he would be snoring away. She lay on the bed facing the ceiling and thinking of what Tristan had said at the table. "So tell me what happened today." She looked up at him as he lay down on the bed and snuggled with her. "They pulled me into a room and questioned me about Tristan's previous diagnosis and our history. A nurse apparently heard Tristan saying something and called child services." Dustin sat up and looked at her annoyed. "And you should of called me," "They wouldn't let me see him or call you till I gave them answers Dustin, they were serious." "Well what happened?" She sat up and swung her feet to the cold floor. "They had three suit and tie guys along with two doctors that I have never seen before. They believe that what Tristan had said was a cry out for help." Dustin wiped his hands down his face. "What was it that he said?" Jody looked at the ceiling for a moment. "They wouldn't tell me Dustin." "What do you mean they wouldn't tell you?" He raised his voice. She turned toward him and pierced her eyes at him. "Please, you'll wake Tristan." He got up from the bed and walked around the room a bit. This was beyond him and knew Jody felt the same way. *Two doctors and three suits, what could they have heard?* "What kind of questions did they ask you?" Jody swung her feet back up on the bed and leaned against the headboard. "About Tristan's school experience, home life, where you and I were from and how our life had been." "Did you call Tolbert's office?" "They already had all of his records Dustin," she whimpered. "They were very serious and said that we will be contacted within a few days for a follow up, I can't understand any of this." Dustin was lost as well and he knew there was more behind this visit. "When are they supposed to be calling?" She got up and walked out of the room and down the stairs. Dustin assumed she was done with the conversation at the moment and did not follow. He sat down on the bed and put his head in his hands. This was something beyond the both of them and he would need to call his lawyer in the morning to find out what can be done to protect them from all of this nonsense. He could hear Jody walking back up the stairs. He fell back on the bed and let his feet swing above the floor. When Jody entered the room he looked over to her. "You ok baby?" She nodded yes and tossed him a card. "That is what the one suit and tie guy gave me before I left to get Tristan. I have never heard of that place and when I called the phone number it went to some voice mail by the name of Dr. Kent." Dustin grabbed the card and sprang up. The card was of very nice quality and the type was a dark embossed with raised font. It read; Department of Medical Development. Jody looked at him and could see he became uncomfortable. "What's the matter?" He placed the card on the bed and stood up. "Nothing, it just doesn't make any sense." She stared at him for a moment and then reached over to get the card. He intercepted, "I have to show this to our lawyer and find out who these people are." Jody walked out of the room and headed down stairs to get a drink. As she entered the hallway she could hear a faint sound coming from Tristan's room just before the stairwell. Stopping by the closed door she moved her hair behind her ear then tilted her head as close to the door as possible. It was quite for at least a few minutes. As Jody went to back up and continue down the stairs Tristan's voice whispered through the door, "Your not listening Jody, do not walk away." She backed up hard and called out to Dustin. He looked out the door puzzled and came out into the hallway, "What is going on?" She pointed toward the door and walked up slowly, gripped the handle hard then swinging it open. Tristan stood on the edge of the footboard facing the door his eyes wide open and staring at his parents with a fury. "They are listening and you are not." He growled. "I will tell you one last time mommy. You will hear us now or we will take him away from you." Jody covered her mouth and backed out of the doorway. Dustin walked up to Tristan and looked up at him from the side. Tristan seemed to be entirely out of it, eyes glossed over, mouth dry. He looked back at Jody and put his thumb to his ear with his pinky to his mouth. She ran back to their bedroom and picked up the cordless phone on her bedside table. As she dialed the hospitals number she could hear Dustin asking him questions. "Who needs mommy to listen?" Tristan looked down at his father and then turned his attention back to his mom entering the room. "Did you think they could help your son Jody?" "They cannot. You do not understand because you chose not to." Tristan balanced on his tip toes and held his fists up toward the ceiling. "We are tired of calling to you Jody and it is time you are taught a lesson." Dustin grabbed Tristan by the waist. Jody yelled, "NO!", and advanced to interfere. Tristan looked down at Dustin, smiled and dropped his arms down. "Daddy," he moaned, and fell into his dad's arms heavy. Jody stopped in her tracks and stared at Dustin as he carried Tristan to the head of the bed and laid him down softly. As he stood up Tristan opened his hand and dropped a quarter to the floor. "They are listening daddy." he whispered. Dustin kissed him on the cheek and looked at Jody. "Is the ambulance on its way?" She shook her head no and walked slowly up to the foot of the bed. "I, I couldn't get a hold of them, they didn't answer, or."

He understood she was in shock from what she had just seen and he walked up to her and took the phone. "Its okay honey, he will be okay." Jody wasn't sure what he meant by that and she only disagreed with the whole thing. How could he just touch Tristan so gently and he comes out of it, snap, just like that. "How did you do that?" Dustin looks her in the eye, now shocked himself. "Excuse me, do what honey?" "How did you touch him like that when we have been told so many times not to? Have you done this before?" He backed his face up a little. "I don't understand what you mean, done what before?" She gripped the edge of her shirt tightly in her hand. "Have you touched him before and not told me?" Dustin smiled, "Honey, I am sorry, I just acted out of fear. I have never tried that before and I am well aware of what I could have done but, the doctor said that things *could* happen. I acted out of desperation and, I, just acted. He doesn't seem to be in any danger." Jody stared at him and looked over at Tristan who was lying soundless, relaxed. Her grip loosened and she put her forehead on his chest. He hugged her and sighed, "Everything will be okay. I will call the doctor in the morning and we will go down there and get some answers." They stood in the room for several minutes before Dustin walked her to the room and laid her down to sleep. Looking at the phone and kissing her on the forehead, placed the phone quietly on the side desk, walked out the room and stood in front of Tristan's door for a few seconds. He shut the door but a crack and walked down the stairs to kitchen to get a drink. Jody lay in bed, eyes wide open waiting for this to all start over again. The kitchen was cold and reminded him of a tomb. Grabbing a cup off the dish rack, he fished his cell phone from his pocket. He looked through his contacts until he found his lawyers number and peered up at the clock, ten seventeen. The thought of calling him this late was already a lost battle as he pushed the quick dial and put the receiver to his ear. As the ring tone echoed in his head he was trying to think of how he would present the situation to John. A scratchy voice interrupted one of the rings, "Hello, John Stathom." Dustin sat for a second, "Hey John, its Dustin Burns. I'm sorry it's late, um, I need you to do me a favor if at all possible?" The phone sat quite for another second or two. "It's ten o'clock at night Dustin, can it wait," "Yeah, yeah, of course. I just need you to look up a company called" he stares at the business card and tilts it toward the windows light, "The Department of Medical Development." John grumbled, "Never heard of it. What is this all about?" Dustin explained to him the situation concerning the suits at the hospital and then the phone call to the Department that led to a Dr. Kent's office." John listened politely and took a deep breath. "Come to my office tomorrow and we will figure out what this is about okay." Before Dustin could respond he heard the disconnection. He sat there in the kitchen and placed the card on the table staring at it. Putting his phone back in his pocket he returned to his bedroom to find Jody sleeping. Taking of his pants he slid between the sheets and rolled over away from her so he could think of what he was going to say to John tomorrow, *Department of Medical Development?* He closed his eyes and slowly wandered into a dream where he stood on his porch and Tristan played in the yard, only two years old. The air smelled like summer and Jody smiled at him as she lounged in a lawn chair and held a glass of lemonade. The fields filled the view beyond the yard that no mans eyes could penetrate. They were safe from the hustle and bustle of the city life and Jody seemed happier. Tristan shook dandy lions in the air and watched the seeds float away as he laughed and grabbed at the grass. The sky was clear, not one cloud for miles and miles. There was an old oak tree on the north end of the lot that must have been there before the house was built. They refused to cut it down although it blocked a great view of the mountains in the distance. As Dustin stared he glimpsed something beside it. He couldn't catch what it was but he squint his eyes as he began to walk towards it. Within three steps he could see it was a figure. "Hey." he called out. The figure held up one hand and everything just froze. His wife in mid drink, Tristan shaking the dandy lion, even the seeds in the air remained still in time. The form just stood there, hand stretched and staring. "Your wife shall listen. You and your son know and understand why she cannot. Make her, or we shall take him." Dustin strained to move and tears burned the creases of his eyes. He sat up in bed suddenly and flopped his feet to the floor taking deep breaths and holding his chest. He went to Tristan's room and found him safely sleeping. Going down stairs he almost fell as he rushed the steps and went to the front door and back around the house. The night air was crisp and stung his nostrils as he fought to catch his breath. The tree stood in the dark, alone. Dustin waited for his eyes to adjust in the dark as he walked slowly towards it. As he approached, the edge of the fields whistled in the soft breeze and filled his nose reminding him of that summer day in his dream. He touched the bark and walked around the tree dragging his hand around with him. There was nothing there. He leaned against the sharp bark and looked out into the fields until darkness blinded him in its distance. Dustin closed his eyes and let the breezed calm him. It would be a big day tomorrow and he would need to have his facts together, Jody expects it. She deserves it and so does Tristan. Dustin opened his eyes with the tree still fresh in his mind. The breeze rushing past his face and the figure he thought he may have seen. Jody was already awake and down stairs with Tristan. They were always up before him and they have grown to understand his pattern. Rolling over, he looked out the window and combed the field. He could do this for hours and sometimes he did. The view was just above the yard line so all he could see was the grass from this height. He could hear Tristan laughing and playing down in the living room. Jody must be in the kitchen getting breakfast cleaned up and thinking about what she needed to do for the day. With that thought he rose from the bed and rubbed his face. He would need to call in to the office so he could go and see John. Dustin got dressed and joined his wife in the kitchen; *I love it when I'm right.* He walked up behind her and hugged her waist as she sipped her coffee. He tucked his chin against her shoulder and felt her smile. "Was this Mitchelle character sporting any ID?" Jody shook him loose, turned around and leaned against the counter. "I didn't see any." Dustin looked around the kitchen then retrieved a coffee cup to join her in the ritual. "I'm just wondering if this guy might have been someone else." Jody slid the sugar down the counter. "Yeah, I can see your point. I should have been more concerned with that." Dustin shook his head. "Nah, I would have been the same way." He began to pour sugar in a heap onto his spoon. After a few spoons Jody sighed, his cue to stop. He stirred with a smile on his face and looked up at her. "I will find out what the deal is and call you as soon as we have some answers." "Anything else you might remember before I go over there?" Jody just smiled and nursed her coffee. "Just call me." Dustin put his cup down and walked into the living room where Tristan was reenacting a Jedi battle, his figures lay strewn across the rug. "Hey pal," Tristan dropped his toys and hopped up. "I'm gonna go to an appointment and when I get back we can go to dinner, k." Tristan smiled and ran into the kitchen to tell his mom the good news. Before Jody could retort to the promise Dustin was already out the door and headed for his car, *typical*, she smirked. Tristan was sent back to the living room so she could finish the morning chores and figure out the day's schedule. Shopping, car wash, call the doctor's office, the list never seemed to end. She could hear the water filling the sink. It didn't matter, not at all. Tristan ran up and down the yard laughing and grabbing at bubbles. He was a porker for sure, that's what grandma used to call him, lil' porker. She couldn't move. Just stood there watching him play in the grass. He seemed to be happy and in those days he was. Dustin sat on a lawn chair watching him and laughing as he sipped his lemonade. She wanted to yell to him, Tristan was running too fast and could fall and get hurt. "You crazy boy", Dustin laughed as Tristan ran in circles chasing bubbles. Dustin would look back at Jody and raise his eyebrows to the middle of his forehead. His big smile looked like a clown about to lose his mind and it made her tremble as she smiled back. "You know Jody," he looked away, "they say you never listen." He looked back at her and ran his fingers through his hair. "Yup, that's what they say." She stared at him blankly, she couldn't move. "I am starting to wonder if they may be right about you Jody. Maybe you just don't listen to anyone, hmmm?" Dustin turned back toward Tristan and raised his hands up in the air like a field goal. "That's it boy, get em! HA, HA. That's my boy!" She didn't know what he was talking about she had always listen to Tristan. "No not Tristan, you dumb bitch." He answered her thought. "Them. The ones in his head Jody." She tried to walk over to him but couldn't move. Tristan stopped in the yard and looked out to the tree. Dustin looked over at him and then back at Jody. "Now look what you have done, you ruined his play time." A tear trickled down her cheek and Dustin gave a disappointed sneer. "That's what we do not need right now Jody. They won't stand for it ya see. Tristan knows this and I know this, why can't you understand that." He got up from his chair and walked over to her and circled around her back. Grabbing her shoulders gently he put his lips to her ear and began to sing softly, "do you hear what I hear, do you see what I see….." He pointed out towards the tree and standing in its shadow some weird figure circled around the back, scrapping the bark. Jody began to panic as Tristan ran towards the tree laughing and looking back at them. She could hear his voice screaming "mommy, mommy!" When her arm was pulled and she snapped her head down, Tristan was standing in the kitchen, water covering the floor. The sink was overflowing and he was panicking as he gripped Jody's arm. She reached over and turned off the sink, scooped Tristan up and held him in her arms. She looked out the kitchen window towards the tree and watched as the wind blew its leaves back and forth. The car ride into town was never the top of the day as far as he was concerned and it made it worse that he was going to see John. He was thankful for anything John had ever done for him and his family but it always came with a long winded story. Last time it was his term as mayor and how the city needed law changes that only someone of his expertise could provide. The radio droned out the world around him and he sang along to almost every song that came on, *all eighties, all the time.* He was hoping that John had some news on these people at the hospital. They had to be state officers for sure but it made no sense to him why they would question Jody like that and then just, let her go? The sun beat down on his windshield and warmed his forearms. He sat back in his seat and relaxed for a bit, it was a long drive into town and he needed all the help he could get to enjoy the ride. As the trees made a strobe light out of the sun he squinted and began to channel surf out of boredom, *only so many eighties songs till ya can't take it no more.* Only a few channels came in here and there. He always found it funny how the country stations, every single one of them, came in so crystal clear and the rest? He just kept on surfing when he heard some news channel and decided to stay with that, *maybe I'll learn something.* Some man was arguing with a Senator about the economic crisis and what it means to them. Dustin was lucky he had a job and thought about what his friends had lost within the last six months, he was very lucky. Coming to this in the middle of heated argument made it imposable to follow their view point and all in all it made boring radio, so the dial found its way into a spin again. A few more country stations and even a light jazz station found its way through, *boring radio.* Just as he gave up all hope in the world of music entertainment, he rolled past a station and caught the loud voice of someone shouting. Laughing, he spun back the knob to regain the channel and began to panic a little when he thought he had lost it, "Son of a bitch," he sat up. He leaned in to focus on the task at hand when a horn broke his concentration. Springing up he jerked his car off to the side of the road, just missing a car as he was heading into its lane. Slamming on the brakes he slid to a stop, gripping the wheel and gritted his teeth. Dust rolled past his window as he looked into his rearview and then out his side mirror at the car as it roared on down the road. He could taste blood from gritting his teeth and he ran his by tongue over his gums while he opened the car door and was greeted with another roll of dust. Standing by his vehicle he took a deep breath and coughed the dirt from his lungs. Looking around for few minutes he walked to the back end of the car and leaned against the trunk. From inside the car he could hear the radio as the man spoke of the glories of heaven. He just smiled and looked at the ground as he strolled up to the door, got in and stared at the radio. Closing the door he fixed his seat, slowly put the car into drive and pulled into the road making sure to check his rear and side view mirrors. He thought about calling Jody but decided this would be a bad idea and she would yell at him for not paying attention in the first place, *no thank you.* The drive seemed to pick up life after the incident and he turned up the radio and listen to the holy man, he felt obligated after the near miss with death. A few minutes into it he realized that it wasn't a preacher but a documentary on myths, legends and lore. Christianity was just rounding up its look at evangelicalisms and Greek lore was finding its way into the conversation. "The gods of ancient Greece were mighty and the powers they had upon their followers were just as heavy." The man barked. Dustin cracked his window and listened as the man continued, "Nothing intrigues a theologian more than that of the underworld." "But what happens to the souls in the underworld?" "They don't care because they're dead." Dustin chuckled to himself. "There are several places in the underworld that souls go before they move on." The voice rolled. "One of these places reminds us that even in the world of the dead there is the idea of human fight for peace. That place is called Elysium fields." He looked down at his watch and compared the time to the travel left. He had only lost fifteen minutes back at the near miss and figured he could make up the time in town by finding a place to park quickly. He only had a half an hour or so left until reaching town, at least the radio had something interesting on. "Elysium was home to heroes as well as the righteous of living. Hercules himself dwelled in Elysium as well as Achilles. After paying their toll the Charon, the toll taker of the river Styx, one could then reach Elysium." Dustin listened as he watched out the side of his window, "The toll of coins." "Coins that the living knew they must poses so the dead would listen." Dustin looked at the radio and then in the review to see if anyone was coming up behind him. He turned his attention back to the radio. The voice said quietly and softly, "Listen to the paying souls wishing to get to the fields. But only the righteous can enter Elysium, only the righteous." Dustin looked out his review again and rubbed his eyes. He realized how tired he was and took a deep breath. Retrieving his cell phone from his pocket and flipping it open as he looked up at the road and then to the radio. The man's voice fading off while he continued with something about Styx and the cost of the toll, he had lost the interest. Flipping his phone open, thoughts raced through his heads about the near accident a mile back and he felt it was time to check in. Jody's voice mail chimed in, "Leave a message after the beep!" you could hear her laughing slightly in the background. "Babe, when you get this call me, I have to ask you a question and it needs to be private, even from Tristan, k. Love you". The remainder of the ride was spent in silence, no theology or news and no eighties flashbacks. John would have probably been able to get the information with no problem, if he hadn't already obtained it somewhere else for someone else. He worked for most of the big wigs at his office and was introduced to John by his boss at a picnic. He would have to be careful what he said around John. Who knew who else he rubbed elbows with and Dustin didn't want his family life to become some barstool conversation at daily grind purging hour. "So they would listen", the stiff voice of the documentary repeated in his head. Is Tristan possessed? Dustin tried to make sense of the thoughts that were running through his head but it sounded foolish. What his son was going through was medical, had to be, and it was hard to put within his head that it could be anything but. Stress does this to people. Reaching for ideas out of desperation. Ghosts, the dead, Greek gods, he sat back and looked to his right, out the window at the sign, "Kemper Falls 25 miles" as he sped past. He wouldn't mention this to John.

CHAPTER 2

The house was built in 1745, by a farmer the deed read. Two story Victorian style with a back porch added by the previous owners in 1982. The original owner liked the Victorian style and made sure the details ran through the entire house. A few renovations had been done before The Burn's had purchased it. A swimming pool put in then removed, a front porch added and removed only a year later. Updated electric in 1996, the list went on and on. The price was a bit hefty and the property a bit large, twenty five acres of nothing but tall grass fields, made them take a month to think on it. No one had put much thought into buying the house and the location being so far from the nearest big town, a forty five minute drive, if you were a lead foot. They had always lived near big cities, Cleveland, New York and even Las Vegas due to Dustin's job and the small town of Elysium Wyoming was quite a change to the family. The job had offered him quite a substantial pay increase to bring his family there and Tristan had only been one year old when they made the move. His condition hadn't started until he was two and for quite some time they had thought it would be wise to move. The company had helped them find a doctor in Rock Springs that understood Tristan's condition so far as they knew it and so they stayed. Besides, Jody was beginning to enjoy the country living and had commented several times how much it was a benefit for Tristan and the family. The only thing that Dustin had a problem with from day one was the odd looking Saw Tooth Oak tree on the north end of the back lot. He thought it looked out of place and was prepared to spend four grand having it torn from its ugly roots. Jody protested saying how she loved the way it complimented the fields and the view of the skyline in the evening, *Friggin Picasso*, he laughed. The only thing that Dustin was given was the choice of windows they would purchase and of course it still had to pass inspector Picasso before the check could be made out. He smiled when he she agreed on the double noise proof pane with the white metal finish, it's what he liked and she just decided to choose the battle wisely. Only one year later while in town, Jody had talked to a lady at the grocery market and found that that lovely tree had been there for several years and was used by the original owner to hang butchered pygmy rabbits, now endangered. Some of the rope was still there and grown into the tree. Jody being an animal lover was horrified by the tale and wanted the tree removed immediately in which Dustin refused by saying, you had your chance, now go watch your sunset Picasso. She didn't speak to him for three days. Dustin remembers the first day that Jody had called him at the office about Tristan. She had been outside with him in the back yard watching him play in the grass. He was fine she said and then all of the sudden he just stood up and looked out over the fields. Jody had figured he had seen a bird or something and was doing what most kids his age would do but after a few minutes he was just too quiet and she didn't feel right. He began to murmur and walk slowly in circles, stopping to stare out into the fields. When Jody had approached him he spun to her and held is hands to his mouth crookedly, "Shhhh mommy." He whispered and sat down in the grass moaning. Scooping him up she ran into the kitchen and was getting her phone to call Dustin when Tristan fled and ran upstairs to his bedroom. She could barely keep up with him and she knew something was not right. He could barely walk that fast especially up stairs and when she reached the top a crash came from his bedroom floor and she watched as he picked up two quarters from his piggy bank now in pieces. Placing them over his eyes he ran his little hands down the side of his face. "Can you hear them mommy?" Jody walked slowly up to him, kneeling and watching. "Tristan honey?" she whimpered. She put her arms out to hug him when he stepped back and scooped the coins from his eyes glaring at her and walking around to the side of his bed. "You should listen mommy, they need you to listen." His voice sounded harsh and controlled, not his. Jody stood up and walked slowly to the edge of the bed. "Who needs to listen sweetie? Tristan, its mommy honey what's going on?" She began to panic. She opened her cell phone and called Dustin making sure to keep all eyes on Tristan as she dialed. When Dustin got on the phone Jody whispered to him, "you need to come home now, it's Tristan. Something is wrong with Tristan." He couldn't retort when he heard the dial tone and ran from the office. Tristan held his hand out to his mother and stared at her weakly. "Why can't you hear them mommy, they are everywhere?" Jody began to raise her voice as she began to cry, "I don't understand Tristan, who! Who are they baby?" He put a coin in his palm and held it straight out to her. He shook from exhaustion and when his hand titled the coin slipped from his hand and Jody reached, snatching it before it hit the floor. "You hear." He smiled. He turned dropping the other coin and she reached missing as it bounced off the floor. Tristan's eyes rolled back in his head as he raised his arms in the air screeching load enough for Jody to cover her ears in pain. She grabbed the other coin squinting as the sound pierced her eardrum rattling her brain. He looked down at her suddenly stopping and looked at the coins in her hand. "You need to listen. We have no time and we will come for him." He collapsed on the floor hitting his head and splitting the skin. Jody dropped the coins and swung him up into her arms and ran from the room, raced down the stairs and left the house with the door wide open. When Dustin finally got a hold of her and found the hospital she had gone to it was three or more hours later. Tristan had a small cut on his head and was sleeping soundly. The doctors were not worried at all and just wanted to monitor him for a bit before letting him go home. Jody did not mention the incident and reported him playing on the bed and falling off. When Dustin had heard the entire story he was confused and just stared at Jody. "Are you sure this is what happened?" She almost took offense but understood how this all must sound to him. "It came out of nowhere Dustin," she continued. "He was playing and then stared out onto the field, and then he just started acting crazy." Dustin sat up, "do you think pesticide could be some of this, I mean they sprayed the fields a week prior Jody?" She shook her head in disagreement and then looked at him, her eyes welling up again. He just held her until they could get their boy and leave. He didn't sleep that whole night and truth be told, he never slept well again. Jody called Tristan from the living room and put his lunch on the table. The water was still coming from under the sink a little and ever towel in the house was drenched on the back porch. *Dustin is gonna be pissed when he sees this.* He came from the living room smiling and looked around for signs of the mighty flood. "Wow mom, you really cleaned that up fast!" She just smirked at him and pointed to his plate and he had no problem responding to the command, "Peanut butter and Jelly!" he cheered. Jody could not understand how that boy could eat that so much? Every time he would act is if it were the holy grail of lunch cuisine. "So, what are we gonna do today?" Tristan bobbed his head back and forth as he chewed his sandwich, "We could go for a walk in the field mommy." Jody smiled and looked out the window at the old tree. "You want to go to town and get some ice cream and do some shopping?" He shook his head yes and continued to attack the crust. That was something she had always been good at. Getting her boys to agree to work needed done all the while they believe that it revolved around fun. Smiling, the back porch called wanting the wet towels to retire to the basement. "Finish your lunch so we can get a move on mister, there is a lot to do." Again, the sandwich holding priority over a response, he nodded in agreement. The basement was always damp but it was the place that the washer and dryer could be stored out of sight. She slapped most of the towels in the washer and just popped opened the cap on the detergent clumsily and began pouring it. From the corner of her eye she caught a shine and something silver in tone sweep back out of her scope of vision. Turning toward the back of the room the dark looked back quietly. "Hello?" she called looking above her head not to be loud enough for Tristan to come, "Who's in my house?" She looked around for something to protect her. Grabbing an old broom from aside the dryer, she held it in front of her. Tristan walked across the floor above her heading for the upstairs. That made her relaxed a little. "Pssst!" she stabbed at the air hoping a raccoon or a cat would run for cover elsewhere. To the left she could see a darker patch than the rest of the room, which seemed to move with the shadows and sway through the particles of floating dust. Jody backed up toward the stairs and turning, she sprinted up to the kitchen and slammed the door behind her. Calling to Tristan, Jody gathered her things and dialed 911. When they left the drive way she stopped down the road, only looking back once and waited for the police to arrive. Dustin arrived at John's office and sat in the waiting room trying to find something to read that didn't include AARP or Fisherman's Quarterly. Many hours have been spent in this office on behalf of Dustin's boss with lawsuits spanning from contractual disagreements, to refunds and payment plans with customers. John was always loud with his opinion of Dustin's system manager position and what it entailed, or what he thought Dustin should be doing. "You're costing the company fortunes by letting these customers tell you what you will do." It was the same spiel every time. His hands became sweaty when he heard John walking down the hallway toward the waiting room, "Hey Dustin, come in." John looked over at the receptionist and pointed at Dustin. "Will you get Mr. Burns here a coffee Melissa?" She left the room with a smile, "She will bring it to the office." He gestured to the door. The waiting room was nice with oak tables and nice paintings. The hallway to his offices had changed a bit though. They used to be beige with certificates of cases he had won and awards that his firm had received from the state. Now the walls were a burgundy color and the wall hangings replaced with shelves and glass cases with collectables and old law books neatly placed. "Yeah," he looked over, "The misses harped me into letting her make my hallway more, professional. Less about the firm's boastings and more about elegance and what she calls", he chuckled, "adult behavior." Dustin just looked around and took it all in. "Don't tell me you have no opinion on all of this Dustin, you must have some personal incite on all of this." He patted Dustin's shoulder firmly. Smiling at John he shrugged his shoulder. "Smart man," John laughed and opened his office door, "pleading the fifth." His office was exactly the same as Dustin remembered it, *She didn't get to the lair.* John circled his desk and sat down adjusting his chair while gesturing for Dustin to sit. Melissa walked in and put the tray of coffee down, "Anything else Mr.Stathom? Mr. Burns?" John shook his head no. "Thank you," Dustin smiled and looked for the cream and sugar. As they fixed their beverage John found his notepad and snatched a pen from the end of his desk. "So, what's going on Dustin?" "What's this about," he picked up a sticky note from his desk, "a, Dr. Kent's and the Department of Medical Development?"

Dustin pulled his wallet and fished the card out tossing it in front of John. "They pulled my wife aside at the hospital and refused to let her see our son until she answered some very personal questions about our business and medical history." John picked up the card and began to jot down information from it to his notepad. "Did they explain what the purpose of the interrogation was about?" Dustin shifted in his seat, "Jody said a young doctor and a nurse had heard him say something in the room and they said they were from the state?" John looked up from under his dark eyebrows, "Well what did they say he said Dustin?" Dustin hesitated and looked at John for a second. John relaxed and lowered his pad. "Look, you called me Dustin, if you are leaving something out or you don't trust me with certain information you might want to take this elsewhere. I cannot help you if you hold information from me." Taking a sip from his coffee, Dustin sat back and looked around the room. "Tristan has a disorder that comes with a few catches. We don't know what it is and the doctor's are stumped as well." John put his right hand up; "I was told by the firm about your son and his seizures Dustin, this is no new news to me. I am sorry but you need to be upfront here so I can get down to business and find out what the hell transpired between your wife and these, officers." "Tristan's seizures cause him to say things that seem as though he has been hurt or is being hurt. We don't understand where it comes from and the hospital was well aware of this condition. It was a new doctor that started all of this." "Are you sure?" John raised his eyebrows a little. Dustin looked up and back down at his coffee, "That's what Jody said had happened." "No", John leaned in, "are you sure it was the nurse or the new doctor that called these people Dustin. Maybe the other head staff had seen enough and decided that Tristan was in jeopardy, in which other means needed to be presented." John sat back and sipped his coffee and then continued. "They have the right to call the state against you if they feel that the child has not been fully treated or taken care of properly. Even against the hospital itself. They are mandated Dustin." This was an idea that in his excitement eluded Dustin and he was sure Jody as well. "So who are these people at the Department of Medical Development?" John took a few more notes and looked up. "The key is getting to know this Dr. Kent and find some type of paper work on the visit. Do I have your permission to do so Dustin?" "Of course John," Dustin agreed nursing his cup. Pushing a button on his phone, John called Melissa back in and told her to get the paper work for Dustin to sign. "Your wife has no problem? Do you want to call her first?" Dustin shook his head no and promised John that this wasn't going to be an issue. "Well, just have her sign the bottom and fax me the back page ok." John shuffled in his desk and pulled out a business card. He wrote on the back and handed it to Dustin. "My other cell number is on their Dustin. It's not for your wife or anyone else. We will keep in touch. Give me a few days to get some info." Melissa walked in and put a packet down on the end of the desk and walked out without saying a word. "The misses hates her", John smiled. Dustin didn't want in that conversation and stood up, shook Johns hand and showed himself out.

Two local police cruisers and one State Trooper vehicle took up more than half the driveway, leaving Jody to park on the grass. They stood outside and discussed their findings with her. Tristan sat in the car and watched, mad that she made him sit while all the action was out there. Jody pointed into the house, "I know that something was in that basement. Did it get out through a window or could it have fled out the back door?" The police did not appreciate the tone and they were about to express this when the State Trooper dismissed them and leaned against his car flipping his pad open asking for her home phone and full name. She gave him the info and he said that a report would be written and if she had any more situations to please call. When he pulled out of the driveway, Jody got back into her car she parked it back in the driveway. Tristan was very quiet and stared out his window. "Honey, I am sorry. If someone or something was in there you could be in danger and no cool police car will replace what I could lose." She leaned down next to him. "The car was really cool though, too bad you couldn't check it out, ha ha." Tristan smiled and then turned to her and pushed her shoulder, "You are mean mommy!" he chuckled. "Yeah, but I still love you." Jody started to kiss his face all over while making loud smooching sounds. Tristan tried to cover his face and curled up into a ball, "Stop, mommy, stop!" They laughed for a minute and then looked out at the house. "What do you think honey, we good in there?" Tristan looked up at her. "I'll take care of you mom", he smirked and puffed up. "Let's go and make some popcorn." Jody smiled and they hopped out of the car and walked slowly towards the front door. Even after the house seemed to be as the police reported, empty, Jody still looked behind her on and off and had an uneasy feeling about the basement. She knew what she saw and when Dustin got home she would go down there with him and have him search that room high and low. Jody left Tristan in the living room and called Dustin's cell phone. It was getting dark out and almost time for dinner. When he answered the phone his voice sounded distant, "What's the matter honey, did everything go ok?" Dustin reassured her that John was going to get some answers but he had to tell John about some personal information about Tristan. He talked about John's ideas with the hospital calling the officers and Jody sat silent. She hadn't thought of that either and kicked herself for it. "I'm fifteen minutes out," the phone crackled, "I'll talk to you then, love you." When she hung up Tristan had finished all the popcorn and was watching cartoons. Jody frowned and rolled her eyes, *piggy*, she chuckled as she walked into the kitchen and opened up the refrigerator to search for dinner. Chicken and rice with green beans and scallions and if time permitted, apple pie. Tristan hated the scallions and didn't think highly of the green beans either. Dustin didn't much care; he liked it all and proved it. Jody just sat and picked, every so often looking up at Dustin and watching the clock. "So," he turned to Tristan. "How was your day lil buddy?" Tristan frowned at his plate. "Mom had the cops come over and she said there was a person in the house!" Dustin looked up at her wide-eyed, "really, hey why don't you go upstairs and get your jammies on and I'll come read you a story okay?" Tristan didn't argue and looked at his food smiling before he took his leave without even a protest. "I was going to talk to you upstairs Dustin, don't give me that look." She said looking down. "What the hell Jody, are you guys okay? Did the police find anything?" She knew he wanted to yell at her but he kept his cool when he saw how scared she was about the whole event. "It was a thing Dustin. I could see it in the back of the room and it was swaying." He sat back, "A thing, like what, a raccoon, a dog, a man?" She put her hands on the table and looked up. "I don't know, I panicked and I….." he interrupted, "its fine, I'm sorry. You must have been scared and with Tristan here." He heard Tristan upstairs slamming his drawers. I will meet you in the bedroom in an half an hour and I will tell you about what John said. We can discuss the basement too, okay?" She smiled and got up and carried his plate to the sink. He looked at the basement door before heading for the stairs and paused to look back once. He felt that maybe she needed him home for awhile. He would request time off tomorrow and they sort things out with John and the doctors. Tristan was lying on his bed with two books and a big grin on his face. "Dad, you should have seen the cars and the lights." Dustin sat down and covered him up. "So, what happened today?" He picked up a book and looked up at his dad. "Mom was in the kitchen and I kept yelling to her. She couldn't hear me and the water was running all over the floor from the sink daddy." Dustin kept his smile on. "Was this before the police came or after." "Before." He smiled opening up cat and the hat and smirking at the pictures. "What was momma worried about bud." He flipped the page. "She said there something in the basement but the police man said nope." Dustin slid onto the bed and backed up to the headboard, took the book and smiled at him. "Are you thing one or thing two my boy!" They laughed and flipped back to the beginning. She finished the dishes and headed up stairs to get ready for bed. In the bedroom she stood by the window and looked down at the tree. She hated that tree and should have taken the chance when Dustin wanted it gone the first time. The yard led to the dark field and out beyond the deep blue hue. The grass swayed slowly and she thought it looked beautiful but at the same time it scared the hell out her. The house felt chaotic with all the activity that was going on lately and she found her bathrobe hoping it would make her feel more secure. She could hear the boys in the background laughing while trying to finish the evening book. Lying on the bed, Jody looked up at the ceiling and thought about what Dustin would come in with. She didn't know John at all and had never really heard too much about him. She was aware he worked for the firm and Dustin was at his office enough to know what he was about and could probably trust him. She thought about the officers and doctors at the hospital along with this Mr. Kent guy. They had given no return call like they promised and she was wondering what the situation was really all about. She felt a little paranoid since the police left. They had looked at her a bit funny and the only thanks go to the State Trooper for holding his breath and having a good nature. *He thought I was crazy.* Dustin walked in the room and stood by the door, leaning against the jam smiling. "He isn't quite out yet so we need to keep it down." He strolled over to the bed and she sat up crossing her ankles. When he sat next to her and placed his hand on her leg she felt a surge of security wash over her. "Well," he took a deep breath. "John thinks the hospital could have been the ones to call and not the staff." She looked at him puzzled. "He said that they are mandated to report when things just haven't worked out they way they think it should, or, if they think Tristan may be in trouble." She gave him a sour look. "They have been observing him for years now Dustin, what the hell could they have seen that would make them think he was in trouble?" Dustin stood up and walked to the window. "His episodes lately have even shocked us Jody. They could have seen something like that. Listen, he didn't say they definitely did, it's just a theory." The sky was making the yard look dead and cold as he scanned the perimeter just to occupy his thoughts. "Well, what do we know about this Kent, and what the hell do they want. They haven't even called back!" Dustin looked at the floor and then turned his eyes up to Jody and smiled a little. "I know I'm frustrated too honey but you got to give John time okay. He will find all this out, Believe me, he is a pit-bull." She fell back on the bed and looked to the opposite side of the room. "I know I just want Tristan to be better." Dustin flopped on the bed next to her and began playing with her hair. "Tristan will be fine and we will figure out what these people wanted." She became optimistic somehow when he talked that way. He the same technique when they had to move here and the stress overwhelmed her. She was glad he had this way with her and she was hoping that he was right.

CHAPTER 3

When John called two days later at noon they were both grinding their teeth and waiting for the story. He seemed pretty confidant of the information he had gathered and hoped that it would clear up a few things for the Burn's. "So John, what did you find out?" Jody looked at Dustin and tried to hear the conversation, leaning her head in and squinting. "Well Dustin, it seems it was the nurse who had called and the hospital only allowed it for record purposes. Mr. Kent is the chief doctor and advisor at the Department of Medical Development. They however are a state funded testing group for medical conditions, how should I say, that are a little strange." Dustin pulled the receiver away from his ear a little, "What do you mean John?" There was a slight pause on the line and he could hear the rustling of paper. "Well it seems that Tristan had said something that made them take notice Dustin." "Were you told what he said?" Dustin squinted. Jody looked at him confused as she tried to listen in. She turned and looked to see if Tristan was listening in as well. She could hear him in the living room having an epic battle keeping him quite occupied. "Well, here is the thing Dustin, I want to make sure you and your wife are prepared for this and you do not take extreme action. Let it sit before you take it to your head too hard. I can, by law, not divulge the information if I think it may cause illegal action." Dustin backed up from the phone again and looked at

29

Jody, his cheeks turning red. "I paid you to find out what the hell is going on John, What the hell is going on!" Jody tapped his arm and signaled him to bring it down. He looked out where Tristan was and took a deep breath. John sat for a second. "Are we clear on this Dustin?" "Yeah," Dustin said calmly, "I just want to know what's going on John." John paused slightly and took a deep breath. "When they brought Tristan to the back, the nurse had come in to check on him, standard activity. Tristan was sitting up and staring at the ceiling, his eyes were rolled back in his head. When she pushed the call button Tristan had looked directly at her and said," he paused a second. "Do not intrude or Ill have his Father kill you. Get the mother." The phone went quite. Dustin was shocked and speechless and Jody covered her mouth looking out towards the living room. "Dustin?" John called. Dustin looked around, "Yeah, um." John reached for a drink on his desk. "Listen to me, I've already put in a request for the records and they have to produce them, at least for you to evaluate." Jody walked out toward the living room and turned the corner to see what Tristan was doing. Dustin rubbed his temple. "Can they take him from us John?" "No, the hospital actually backed you up and said that his condition was being studied and that he has never nor have you two shown any signs of harm or danger." Dustin felt hopeless and rubbed the phone against his ear. His eyes welled up and he tried to breath differently to cover it up. He was interrupted by a scream from the living room. Jody backed out from the room and reached her hand back toward Dustin. He turned and lowered the phone flipping it shut. "Jody?" he went to her, grabbing her shoulder. Tristan was standing on the coffee table naked and his head rolling toward the ceiling. His clothes seemed to have been torn from him, lying in a heap on the floor next to his action figures. In his hands he had two quarters, rubbing them between his fingers, "Tristan?" Dustin moved to the side of him within two feet. He just stood there, eyes rolled back and chanting some strange moans. Jody stood by the door way and watched, frozen. Her eyes began to water, she couldn't blink and fear began to rise in her chest. Tristan's skin was clammy looking and he was breathing deeply. Dustin wouldn't touch him but walked around analyzing what he was seeing, "Tristan, are they here?" His son didn't respond verbally but began to sway left to right slightly. "We are listening Tristan, are they listening?" Tristan looked down at his dad and smiled. "Why do we need to go through such great lengths for you to listen? We have been trying to show you for years yet now you still do not listen." Dustin put his hand near Tristan but pulled away slightly when he almost made contact. "I do not understand," Dustin trembled. "Why do you need my son? What do the dead want with my son?" Jody stared at Dustin, *what?* Tristan rolled his eyes back down and looked around the room. "We are ages old, we are never dead. There is no death boy's father." Dustin walked to the front of Tristan, "What do you know about Elysium fields?" Jody put her arm out. "What are you doing Dustin?" She trembled. He looked over at her and held his arm up signaling her to wait. She covered her mouth and shook with panic. He continued, "Elysium fields, what is Elysium Fields?" Tristan looked around the room. "It is a place of human intervention, were your gods live and the righteous dwell. Do you want to see the field boy's father? Or should we take the mother?" He looked in Jody's direction eyes wide. She backed up more and looked at Dustin. "No Tristan," Dustin held his hand up, "we do not need to see Elysium, what is it you want us to do? Why are you here?" Tristan raised his hand and showed the coin. "This is why we are here." Dustin was lost and looked at Jody, "The coins?" Tristan opened his mouth and held his hand out letting the coin teeter on his palm. His eyes widened and he let out a horrible screeching sound that almost dropped them to their knees. Jody covered her ears as she looked over to Dustin who backed away in pain clasping his head. Tristan walked off the table and out toward the kitchen. Dustin followed clasping his head in pain, trying to grab a hold of Tristan as he walked right out the back door. Birds shot out from the tree and field as Tristan headed down toward the end of the yard, screeching, palms straight out. Jody ran for the back door watching Dustin stumbling in the yard as he tried to stop his boy. The grass parted like for Tristan as he entered, his face pointed up, hands out and protruding these high-pitched calls from his lungs. Mice, snakes, rabbits and insects crawled up onto the yard to escape the howl, climbing over one another ignoring the food chain. Jody collapsed to the porch and stared at the swarm of beasts running from her son, pressing her palms to her ears. Dustin got balance and ran after his son plugging one ear, walking unbalanced. Tristan never looked back and seemed to hover through the grass. Jody watched the creatures disappear under the porch and around the side of the house. She tried to catch her breath but her panic overcame her and she sat watching Dustin following their son into the field, deeper and deeper. They were being swallowed by the horizon and the screeches faded with every passing second. She looked around in shock, her eyes glossed and with a deep breath she lowered her hands. Lying down, her eyes felt heavy. The last sound she heard was the distant screech and the wind as it blew past her face. She closed her eyes. Jody held Tristan so tight when the nurse gave him to her she thought he would suffocate. He was a good eight pounds one ounce and huge blue eyes with only a little tuft of hair to speak of. Dustin was taking pictures and Jody's Mom and Dad were trying to squeeze in a little grandparent time but Jody would have no part in it. Even Dustin was shunned when he went in for the grab. He just smiled and waited his turn knowing she would fall asleep eventually and that would be his moment of victory. They had planned his birth for months trying and when she found out she was pregnant; Dustin just fell in love all over again. When he got his big job offer they spent the earlier weeks of Tristan's life finding out just where it was they would be moving. Time flew by as Jody thought about when Tristan had lost his first tooth, it was traumatic for him but Jody and Dustin couldn't help but laugh. It had been damaged when he had fallen at ten months old and they were told not to worry, it fall out eventually. When it did, Tristan ran screaming through the house. He wasn't in pain at all but just to see it fall out put him into frenzy. Jody held him and smirked at Dustin who tried as hard as he could not to smile back. She remembered his first birthday party, his first play date and his first seizure, memories flashing by. Jody opened her eyes and fuzzy grey and white border filled her vision. It was quite where she lay and the smell of summer filled the air. Her head wasn't clear enough to grasp were she was but it seemed so comfortable and familiar. When the room became to come slowly into focus Jody could see the wall and as she looked up, the window giving views the back yard skyline. She slowly sat up and began to breathe heavily when she remembered lying down on the porch as Dustin and Tristan went into the field. It was impossible to call out and she pushed back the sheets to get up. She opened her mouth and tried to call for them but her throat felt as if someone had torn it out. It burned every time she swallowed and when she turned her head, what *the hell happened to me? Where is Dustin, my son?* There was a loud ping that tore through her head. Jody fell back and stretched her mouth so wide she thought it would tear. Her eyes began to burn and her body quivered and a scream echoed through her skull. "We know where your Tristan and Dustin are Jody". She began to panic as the voice burned in her temples. "Listening was your goal from the beginning of this venture." *What is this?* She pulled at her hair. "Listening is the entire key we need. We are aware that this has become the fight since the first days." *Who are you, where is my son, where is my husband?* The voice boomed through her head making her wince, "Tristan and the man are not with you anymore, they are with us. It was the boy who had brought the man here." She tried to sit up and her muscles shuttered at every move. *How are they with you? Who are you, please?* "We are the watchers, the ones your son has called." The room began to fill in with a ring of dark fuzz. Jody began to breathe heavily and her body became stiff. "Relax Jody, we will show you of your Tristan." Before she could respond she was slammed in the head with a load boom and she felt her body fall from the bed onto the floor. Her blood boiled and her skin blazed as scenes of the basement filled her mind. Tristan sat on the floor while she did laundry, the sun beaming from the stairwell leading to the kitchen. Tristan was preoccupied with his toy soldiers and she could hear Dustin in the yard swearing at the lawn mower, which became a standard weekend occurrence. "Surrender if you understand our demands!" Tristan shouted. Jody just smiled and continued to fold the linens. Tristan stopped suddenly and stood straight up starring into the corner of the basement. By the time Jody had noticed him he was staring long enough for his eyes to pour tears down his cheeks. "Tristan?" she could remember calling. He stood silent and as she approached she could see, in the vast darkest corner of the basement, something writhing. "Hello?" She grabbed Tristan by the arm and slowly tried to turn him away. His head turned as far as his neck would let him before he blinked and then went full blown into a seizure, swinging at his mother and screaming, "Do you hear them? They want you to hear them!" She scooped him up the best she could and headed for the stairs calling to Dustin who remained oblivious to the situation at hand. *This was not his first seizure.* The voiced echoed as it faded into her head, "But this was the first that he came to them for the answer." "We told him to have you listen to us, not to the beast in the basement. We are stuck here and we have no need for this place any longer Jody." *Then what are the seizures from?* "We do not know but it is our way in, as we are here with you now. You have this condition we need as well. Do you not remember?" Jody began racing through thoughts trying to connect all of this together. She knew for the first time that they were not here to do harm, at least not now. They had her in this position for quite some time and nothing has happened up till this point, except for the field. *Where are they? Why the field? Why did Tristan go to the field?* "It was not the field we called him to, it was the place we have met before." *before?* She responded. "Yes, before, others like you as far back as we can remember Jody." *Where is this before?* "In the corner you hated since you have arrived on our plantation." *The tree?* "Yes". We will send Tristan to get you. We believe you must listen first to understand where it is we need to go, we are lost." *I need Dustin. The man?* "We cannot give the man. We have no way to do this, although we wish this could be given to you." *Why? Why can't you give me the man?* "He is in the field were the boy had left him." "We will allow you to go and see and then you will find your Tristan and listen to us." As fast as the pain had entered Jody she sat up, blood squirting from her nose, which she now realized, was nearly broken. She leaned up against the bed and tried to focus her eyes, the room was bright and her head began to pound. Stumbling to her feet she made her way toward the stairs and held onto the rail tightly, wobbling down toward the living room. Slowly the room stopped throbbing and she could make full sense of where she was. Her head still throbbed but was passing just the same. The kitchen was attacked by sunbeams from the window and the back door was wide open. The cupboards were ravaged and food lay scattered throughout the kitchen. She knew that it was from the fleeing animals that stopped to eat when they realized the opportunity before them. *How did I get upstairs?* She went out the back door and looked to the edge of the yard into the field. Small patches snaked its way through the grass were Dustin went after Tristan the day before. Jody looked down at herself realizing that she had on the clothes from last night and took a deep breath as she walked to the yards edge. The tree swayed back and forth and seemed to dance to her footsteps, watching her gather strength to enter the field. She paused, looked out and scanned the field as far as her eyes could manage. *Where are you*

Dustin? The grass began to move apart as she entered. Jody stopped and spun around as the grass closed behind her as if to warn of no return. The wind blew past her ear and she could hear the faint sound of birds in the distance. Suddenly she could smell Tristan. Jody looked around frantically, "Tristan!" she bellowed. "Honey, where are you, its mommy!" She began to follow the smell deeper into the field not bothering to look back towards the house. *He was here in the field and they were leading me to it.* Her nose began to bleed heavily and run down her face splattering on her shirt as she began to pick up speed through the grass. "Baby, just tell me where you are. I'm here Tristan!" *You won't keep him from me. If you want me to listen you won't keep him from me.* The horizon showed no sign of giving up and the field returned the promise with a sea of yellow in the distance swaying back and forth. Jody stopped and bent over trying to catch her breath. Looking back for the first time in several minutes the house looked like it was a mile away. The tree still danced and mocked her as the wind brushed its leaves. She looked around for a second and took in distance. She couldn't see were Dustin could have gone to and were Tristan left him. There were no hills, no old houses, nothing. She began to walk again and scan the fields for signs of any kind. A few birds shot out from the brush and startled her, holding her chest she noticed something odd. Tristan's smell was no longer with her. Had she went too far, did it veer off somewhere? Looking to her left she could see, about fifty feet away or more, a small clearing in the field. She sharpened her eyes, *Dustin?* She ran almost tripping as she stumbled through the grass. When she came up to the clearing Jody fell to her knees and held her mouth. Dustin lay in the far edge of the fifteen foot clearing. His face down in the dirt and blood seeping into the ground around his forehead. She crawled to him and realized that he was stiff from being there the entire night. His body was hard and seemed to be encrusted to the ground as she pulled to flip him over. His face was bashed in making his face hard to recognize. The blood pools trailed off, disappearing into the field. A large tree limb was found several feet away from Dustin's dead body, covered with blood. Jody sat back and wiped her hand on her pants, panicking and in complete shock. "Tristan!" she screamed, "Tristan!" again and again until she could taste blood in her throat. Sitting in the field she screamed for him over and over. The sea of grass mocked her and the tree danced to the symphony of her screams. It had lost a limb but rejoiced at its message. Listen.

The house was cold and the night air seemed to rip at the walls of the house to tear it down. The walk back from Dustin's grave gave Jody time to think about what was happening. She wanted to call the police but knew they would be of no help and would only take her away from the home. She walked into the house and shut the doors, turned up the heat and cleaned what she could of the kitchen. It was giving her time to contemplate where Tristan was and what they needed her to do. The voices had not come back since she entered the field. She asked for them several times during the walk but they ignored her. Her head still throbbed and was accompanied by a painful throat. Jody took what she could from Dustin's corpse, the cell phone, his wallet. When she had finished cleaning the damaged kitchen, Jody went to the living room in the dark and sat on the couch lost. What was going to happen? *Is this it? Please give me my son.* She looked through Dustin's wallet, hoping for something, some kind of sign that he knew something she did not, nothing. His ID, a few credit cards and some business cards from the office, some coupons from a restaurant. She put everything on the coffee table and picked up his phone turning it on. As the light filled her face in the darkness she noticed he had some messages. Activating his message service there were three, all from last night. One was from his uncle in Washington, she skipped it not bearing to think of what she would tell them when this all came to light. The second was a hang up, which didn't sit well with her. Then a familiar introduction came over the speaker. "This is John Stathom, Dustin I have some pretty weird news about your boys at the hospital. Turns out they were there on behalf of the state to take your boy away. Seems you guys have forgotten to mention to me the incident when your son attacked his mother. Please give me a call back and let me know what I'm supposed to do here Dustin, you got me in quite a tight pinch here, Talk to ya soon." The click startled Jody in here daze and she set the phone down, got up and headed for the kitchen again. She needed some water and to find something for this god awful throbbing. The kitchen, although cleaned a little, seemed dingy and dead. The whole house felt this way to her as she looked out the window towards the field. Scanning her eyes met with the tree. The tree, she slammed her glass on the counter and headed out the back door. The grass in the yard was moist and the night air bit her cheeks. The tree swayed in the night dancing as it always did. "What have you done with my son?" She pointed. It swayed ignoring the question. Jody became angrier and looked around the yard. "You my friend have seen your last days on this property! Tomorrow men will come here and you will be ripped from your foundation and cut into pieces from me to burn in that goddamn field!" She stomped back and forth, "Tell me where my son is, they said it was you!" The tree swayed and the breeze moved the leaves as if to answer, but she knew it didn't listen, couldn't listen. *Where are you?* A loud ping ripped through her head and she collapsed onto the grass. "You have found the man?" a voice sifted through the pain. *Why did he do this to his father?* There was a slight pause as the pain slowed and she regained function to her body, "We did not tell your son to do this. The man you called the father or Dustin would not let him come to us." Jody sat up and brushed her hand over her head. *What is it you want?* Tears began to fill her eyes and she fell onto her side and rolled into a ball. "We need you to listen," she cut them off with a scream, *I have fucking listened time and time again!* There was silence as she wept in the yard. "We need the answer for the master, where are the coins that the son has used to call you? You never answered before but now, you come to us. Was it the coins that pushed you away?" Jody was confused and just held her head letting out bellows ignoring the ramblings of her demanders. "Your son will come to you tomorrow and you will listen then." *What is the tree?* The voices went silent. *What is the tree?* A boom set off into her head and the voice multiplied by what seemed to be a million. "You shall receive Tristan and he will show you the way to us. We have limited time." Jody curled tighter, pushing her knees into her chest. The world around her gave off sparks of light and her mind burned through her eyes. A metallic taste filled her mouth and she gave a slight whimpered before all went black again. The breeze pressed her hair to her face as the grass coddled her body. Her world was silent and the only thing she could hear was the faint sound of Tristan calling her name. The field was damp and the ground squished around his feet as he parted the grass. His father lay, crumpled in the corner of the circle and to Tristan, he looked to be asleep instead of dead. A tear welled up and trickled down his left cheek as he stood staring. Wiping it away, Tristan looked out towards the house in the distance. There were no signs of his mother or any other life. It just looked like a painting in the background meant to calm him for the time being. His pants were a little dirty and his shirt torn at the bottom a bit. Tristan didn't seem be aware of anything except the field as it stared back at him coaxing him forward toward the house. The grass swayed in its direction like finger directing him, "come". As he entered the grass it parted and made his way easier. *What do you want me to do?* The only answer was the wind as it blew in his ear tickling his face. Some crows made their presence as they flew from the brush in the distance, cawing as they fled. He made little of the event and looked towards the house to see if any sign of life, even if it were a silhouette in a window, nothing. Occasionally he would look back towards the clearing with a dreaded thought of his dead father rising to take vengeance. He could picture him running through the fields towards him with his arms stretched out, his bloody face contorted and maimed. *Why did you make me kill my father?* The ground seemed to hum and the background shook a little as the voice filled his head. "We did nothing to your father Tristan. It was he who tried to stop you and you who took the actions." Tristan stopped abruptly and put his hands to his face and sat down in the grass slumping to one side, *that's a lie!* He sobbed. "Oh it is not. We didn't interfere with what your plans were for him. It is not our place to tell the listener what he is to do." He looked up at the sky hoping his eyes would roll back into his head so he could speak to the voice face to face. *That is a lie!* "It is not a lie." They whispered, "We cannot stand in your way and you will do what it is you want without our demands." *Where is my mother?* There was a slight pause. "Asleep in the grass Tristan, waiting for you." *In the grass, Why?* The voice faded almost completely and he could sense that for the first time it was careful on its response. Tristan stood and dried his face with his hands, *why?* He repeated. The voice faded out and then burst in with a load slam in his skull forcing him to the ground in pain. "We do not control the place of your mother. We grow tired of the questions. You will go to her and make her listen or we will go to her ourselves and she will listen whether she desires to or not!" Tristan looked towards the house and could see the wind blowing in a path towards the house, pushing the grass to the side as it snaked on without him. He stumbled to his feet and began to run after it ripping through the grass, trying to keep up. The house seemed to be millions of miles away and his lungs were burning as he pushed on. The wind would swirl up as if to look back and laugh before it descended into the field and continued on. *Stop please! I will speak to her, I promise!* He stopped in mid stride and put his hands to his knees as he spit phlegm and took deep breaths. The wind just sped forward ignoring his plea. Tristan knew his mother would be in danger and stood up looking towards the yard in the distance in hopes to see where his mother was laying. The grass was too tall and the wind was too fast. He began to jog towards the house again with his lungs on fire and his eyes watering with pain. *Dad, I need you.*

CHAPTER4

The office was empty for once and John Stathom was bored. He kept thinking of what he was going to do on vacation this year since he had been everywhere he ever wanted to go. He looked around the room and ran his hand across his leather chair. His eye caught a cigar he had left in the ashtray on the windowsill and sprang to get it. The outside world looked cold and even though his office wasn't much of a scene to behold, he liked it here better where no one could pester him. The room began to fill with the smell of Cuban royalty and John peeked out the window, looking down the yard to the streets, finding nothing that interested him more than puffing on royalty. Blowing smoke around as if he was making sure the entire room carried his beloved odor he walked back towards his desk and look down at a vanilla folder under his cell phone. "Dustin, he shook his head, why haven't I heard anything yet bud?" As much as Dustin had called and drove all this way bugging him about the hospital incident he thought that he would hear back instantly when he called with the info? He picked up his phone and flipped it open, no messages. He began to scroll through contacts and finding what he was looking for, pressed send taking a puff of his cigar. A cute voiced woman answered the phone and John went right into mister Sauvé mode, he could picture his secretary chuckling every time he did this. "Yes I'm looking for a Dustin Burns?" She put him on hold and he took the opportunity to head to the counter by the door and pour himself a shot of Jack Daniels. This is something that happened frequently throughout the day and he was sure he should buy stock but never had. He was enjoying the smell of his cigar and the sharp jab of Jack when she clicked back, "I'm sorry, Mr. Burns is out sick, may I take a message?" John put his glass down. "This is John Stathom," "Oh, she interrupted, I'm sorry Mr. Stathom, I wasn't aware it was you. Mr. Burns was supposed to report back to work two days ago and we have made several calls but have received no response of any kind." John frowned, "Has anyone made a trip out to his home?" She paused for a minute, "I don't think so sir, would you like one of the managers paged?" John took a breath and looked around the room, "That's okay, I'll go there myself. Just inform the company I'm taking a trip and if they need me to call my cell, not my office okay sweetie?" He had to add that to keep his role up. "Thank you", she said with a shy tone, he loved that. When he hung up the phone he looked toward the desk at the folder, "What the hell are you doing Dustin?" He walked back over to the window and dialed Dustin's cell. It rang a few times then he heard the message click on. He shook his head and began to pull the phone away from his ear as a faint voice called out to him, "listen" it whispered. John put the phone back up to his ear, "John?" The phone was dead. When he called it back he got the answering machine again and this time he left a message. John put out his cigar, finished his shot and grabbed his coat as he headed out the door. It was grey outside and the long drive would give him time to think of other things, like Dustin and his family. The company was ready to count Dustin as a loss at this point and John wasn't interested in politics and bullshit at the moment. It was far beyond that and he was quite sure whatever was going on Dustin wasn't concerned with the welfare of his employment. The trees caught John's eye as he looked out the window watching cars pass as well as the occasional house, *what the hell was going on Dustin?* While reaching for the knob to the radio he wiped some dust of the dash, "why do I pay these schmucks?" twiddling his fingers in the air. Like usual he went through quite a few channels before he found anything worth noting. He had never taken the time to set the dials to his favorite stations they would just get screwed up when the car detailers took it every week. Fishing his cigarettes out from his side jacket pocket he rolled down the window a crack and sat back to get comfortable, it was going to be quite the drive. He thought about the guys in the hospital that Dustin was concerned with and tried to tie them into this more but found it a dead idea every time it ran through his head. Stathom checked his pack of smokes and realized that a chain-smoking event may occur, *Time to find a corner store out here in Boonsville and get acquainted with the locals.*

Stepping into the yard Tristan could feel the house staring him down, "Mom?" he called. The wind brushed past his face and he jumped waiting for the swirl to show up again and topple him. They voices seemed to have left and a void in his mind was evidence of the departure. "MOM?" he yelled louder as he walked slowly to the back porch. A few snakes made their way past him from under the wood slats making sure to avoid him. Tristan looked back at them as they disappeared into the field and he knew that the voices must be with him in some instance for the snakes to act that way, *where is my mother?* The wind on the branches from the corner tree was the only answer he received. He stared at the tree for a moment and began to walk towards it as if drawn. The limbs swayed back and forth and bent in as if they wanted to hold him and show him that he was safe here. Tristan knew better than to trust anything at this point and approached the tree with caution. As he got within a foot of the giant it seemed to look down at him and smile through the rough grain of the bark and the leaves tried to whisper secrets, "We have been waiting for you to find us here Tristan." He looked to his feet and felt his head get dizzy. "We know you are upset about your father and we understand you cry for your mother. We don't want you to cry any longer Tristan. All you need to do is set us free. Get the coins from her and bring them to us, then the world will listen." Tristan felt his body lump to the ground and he tried not to panic as the grass brushed his cheeks and hugged his body, *what is it you want, why the coins?* "It pays our way to the others, we were hung here by the master." Tristan pursed his lips and tried to bring himself out of the coma, "He brought us here one by one in the night and hung us from the arms of nature with chains and rope. The Fathers were first and then the mothers." The tree began to bend and creek violently as Tristan opened his eyes, looking up at its evil hardened face he was released from the coma. Leaves blew out into the yard and he began to crawl towards the porch hoping the tree would not intrude, "Bring us the coins Tristan or we shall hang your family from the very tree that drank our blood, like your father!" He stood up and ran for the back door as the tree swung back and forth throwing leaves and dead branches across the back yard. Birds and animals scurried into the field and the house itself moaned in fear. As he opened the back door and slammed it hard behind him, silence filled his pounding ears. He walked, crouched, to the kitchen window and climbed up on the sink to look out at the beast. The yard was still and silent and the only proof of the fury was the slowly swaying tree and the debris strewn throughout the back yard. He climbed down and looked around the kitchen and realized that it was pretty well tattered itself. He could tell someone had attempted to reorganize it but didn't finish the job, knowing it was a worthless venture, *mom*? The hallway to the living room was clouded with dust and it caught up in his throat as he brushed the air with his forearm, making his way into the room, "Mom?" The room echoed and pulled the sound to the depths of the house making him feel uneasy and giving no reply. Tristan understood the tension throughout the house and knew it was them. They controlled every aspect of time, thought, movement, life. They wouldn't let go until they made people listen, that was what this was all about from the beginning. He tried to remember back when the voice had first come to him and found it was barely reachable now. He could feel himself lying in bed when he was 4, maybe younger, and as he would slip into sleep they would whisper to him, "Can you hear us?" It scared him at first as it would anyone he supposed, but something told him to listen, relax, they were here for a good purpose. The voices grew after the first few visits. By the time he had reached five they had taken over most of his time with questions about his mom and dad, when they would hear them and could he help make them listen. He felt bad for them and sometimes promised he would find some way to help them escape were ever it was they were. The first doctor visit was a nightmare and they did nothing but ask odd questions about what it is he had heard in his head. He tried to tell them that it wasn't just his imagination and they weren't hurting him in anyway, they just needed someone to listen, but to what he wasn't sure. That was the question that he could remember asking himself over and over again in the years that passed. They never really answered him and it felt as if it was as if he never had permission to know. That should have been the first clue that this wasn't what he was led to believe. They had an agenda and at this point Tristan knew it couldn't be anything that would benefit him. When he tried to break off communications two years ago is when the serious hospital visits came into play. He could remember trying to push them out and they would just knock and knock until his brain felt it would split. Without any warning his body would just tense up and he could feel his mind burning. When he came to it was always the same story, he could remember everything but was self warned that telling would not be in his best interest. Doctors would never believe him anyway. The stair case was clouded and he could only see half way up, "Mom?" *Where is she?* The house groaned a bit when he put his foot on the first step, Please *give me my mother and I will tell them to listen,* he paused and waited for a response. After a few minutes he felt relieved that they, for once, didn't occupy his head. He also knew that this wasn't necessarily a good thing either. Slowly he took a few steps up the stairwell and tried to look beyond the corner, through the dust. Everything was just too quiet and why did his mother not respond. *Did I kill her too?* The field was bare. No tall blades of grass, no bird calls. Even the sky gave off a dull hue and seemed to want her to leave and never return. She wasn't sure how she got here in the first place, *where the hell is this?* Walking in a circle, the empty field went for miles until the eye couldn't make out anything recognizable. There was no sun but the sky looked like mid afternoon greeting the night shift and ready to retire. Jody looked down and realized that the grass had been burnt down. It was black but not sharp like she felt it should be. It was quite soft and gave off a poppy odor that made her breath slower and began to calm her. The air also seemed thick and sticky as she took a deep breath and scanned the horizon again, *where am I?* Her mind seemed to be clouded a bit and found it hard to concentrate on anything. As she began to walk again her knees began to buckle. Catching herself on one knee, she sat down and looked at the blackened grass. Her brain began to shot fire down her spine and she looked up knowing as she awaited them to come into her. Jody held her breath and looked toward the horizon. A fuzzy silhouette began to fade into view ahead. She tried to clear her mind, to concentrate, but the fire shot bursts down her spine again, crippling her to the ground. "What do you want!" she cried. Just when she thought she would pass out the pain surged one last time and left her drooling on the grass. She felt a hand touch the top of her head and slowly run down to the back of her neck. Jody breathed lightly and could feel her body melt. She knew that touch. She could remember it from the very first time she had ever felt it. As Jody looked up slowly, Dustin smiled back down at her. Her heart raced and she slowly rose to her knees and looking up at him. His body had a strange glow to it like fog had wrapped him instead of flesh. His smile had a twist to it making him appear insane, but loving. His eyes flashed fire and seemed to light up everything within two feet of them. She could barley look straight into them without squinting. Dustin walked around her and held his hands in the air, "Do you know where we are Jody?" His voice echoed across the fields and shook the ground. She slowly stood up and stared at him smiling. "I don't know." She said quietly. Dustin fixed his clothes, which Jody just realized he had on under the fog. It lifted as he brushed and returned to engulf his body, hugging it. "This is the place where all that is glorious finds its way to then end. This is the halfway point and the time we wait for those to listen." Jody could hear Tristan's rants in his voice, "Listen for what?" Dustin stopped walking and stared at Jody with his upper teeth showing, "For the way, for the answer." He reached into the fog and brandished a coin. The silver edging let off rays of light that made a bubble around him making his teeth look hungrier. He flipped it in his palm and held it out to Jody. She just stood and stared at his hand, "What is this?" she looked into his eyes. Dustin walked towards her and she stepped back a foot tilting her body further away. He put it near her face and got his mouth within one foot of hers. His breath reeked of death and for the first time Jody could see that none of this monster standing before her was her Dustin. "This is the payment through Jody. This is what the toll man desires to get through but he's nowhere to be found." He quickly snatched his hand shut and spun away from her walking a few feet away, his back facing towards her. "You know, Tristan is a very smart boy Jody and he has found a way for us to get through." He turned his head slightly to show the side of his cheek, "You just needed to listen." Behind him the house appeared and seconds after the yard and the sky. He turned towards her and smiled widely. Jody scanned the mirage and noticed one thing missing. "This isn't real Dustin." He turned his head looking at the house, "why do you say that?" The yard was clean and the wind blew some of the ornaments hanging on the back porch. She wanted to believe that this was real, "The tree, where's the tree?" He gave out a small chuckle. "This is why I married you sweetheart, you are quick. The tree, well…" he raised his hands and the beast appeared and came, leaning forward, swaying back and forth in the wind, reaching for Jody. "A lot of people have died on this tree, it has a long history with us." He sneered, "With you." Jody took another step back as she watched the tree lean in for a closer look. "See the master that owned this house had quite the collection of humans. You refer to them as slaves, yes? Jody looked away. "Well," he continued, "he hung them from that tree when they could do no more for his precious fields and realized what these fields really were." He walked around her and looked at the ground is if he had lost something. "That tree has more history than you or I shall ever have Jody. Those people think they need to be set free." "What were the fields?" she turned to him. "Well that's just as it sounds. They were his crop," he chuckled. "He was a farmer Jody, but see the fields, they watch over the tree to make sure it stands tall and keeps those souls within its grasp. They cannot go on when they cannot pay the toll." "Is that why Tristan is bringing you the coins?" Dustin stopped and stood staring at her. It felt as time had stopped and he was frozen, just glaring at her. It made her look away slightly. "You just don't like to listen, or think for that matter. The coins will bring you and the child to the fields for the toll keeper, but we will not have ownership of the coins, we will pay with you and the boy. Two very well grounded souls for many wanderers." He put his hand out and the tree swooped down and grabbed Jody flinging her into the air."

CHAPTER 5

The scenery was beginning to get to him as he watched the trees and the road taunt him with the same view minute after minute, *This is why I never come out this way John.* He began to search for his pack of smokes he had just purchased from a mom and pop store not twenty minutes earlier. That was something that always bugged him about the country life. Everything was mom and pop for the most part and it made him sick. *How could everyone know everyone else and why would you want to? Who the hell cares why the local church is holding their annual "food drive for the community".* He liked his city life and he liked his solitude within it. That was what he found relaxing, the fact that not one single person knows the other and if they do then they don't discuss it or show much of it unless you had a good reason. He was known for his grumpy attitude towards people and although he was awarded several accomplishments for the community, to him that was a career stabilizer and that was it. So why then did he find himself driving all the way out into the remote sectors of the world to find out what happened to an employee of a company that he handled? Cause for some reason he liked Dustin and his family. He had seen Dustin at many company venues and seen several pictures and heard many stories of Tristan and Jody that he felt that he had known them personally. He had spoken to Jody once or twice but by no means did he consider it "friends". But wh the hell is going on with an employee that dedicated his life to this company and then suddenly, BOOM he's gone. Now his gut told him that Dustin was probably sick and the stress from everything got to him, so in turn, time off. His head told him that even if that were the case, he would have at least phoned in and told the company of his plans to take several days off. He lit a cigarette and cracked his window to let in some clean air. Looking out the window he thought of several other reasons he had and rolled his eyes at the passing trees, *Jesus.* The bedroom smelled like hot paint and it burned his eyes and tongue. The dust wasn't as thick up there and he could see in the room pretty good as he shuffled around looking for Jody. The window let in streaks of light that pushed the dust aside which also helped him to make things out. When he walked up and looked out the window, he could see the back yard and the tree, which twisted and bent down with the wind with an evil dance. He wasn't sure why the tree hated so much but he thought it was more they then the tree. They wanted everyone to listen and this was how it was going to be done. Tristan sat on the bed and looked around the room. He felt calm as he remembered lying there with his mom and dad, playing and rolling around. Dad would tickle him on his chest and he would curl up in a ball trying so hard not to cry out but his dad always won that war and Tristan would scream so loud the walls would shake, "Stop! You win, you win daddy!" His mother would stand in the door way and scold Dustin for what he was doing to her precious Tristan and then would come and scoop him up like a baby, laugh and walk out the door leaving Dustin to think about what he just did. Tristan curled up on the bed and began to cry softly. What had he done to his father? Why would he have done that to him in the field? He loved his dad so much and couldn't believe they would make him hurt him. "Oh, it's okay son", Tristan sat up quickly. He looked to the door way and could see a silhouette blocking the hallway view, "Dad? The figure held out his arms and Tristan stood up and ran, slamming into him and gripping his waist. The fog around him just wisped away for a second and then engulfed them again, "Ah Tristan, Did you miss me?" He looked up at his dad and smiled and tried to see through the fog that covered his face. The man leaned in an as the fog split and Tristan saw the distorted twist in the man's smile, his eyes glowing and staring ·traight into his. He knew this wasn't his father. He backed up and bumped against the bed putting his hand back to steady himself, "What's the matter son, its daddy Tristan?" Tristan shook his head no and watched carefully what the stranger was about to do. The man walked past him and looked out the window to the tree. He spun and stared, "So, it's come to this has it?" Tristan stood silent. "Well, your mother is looking for you and they are waiting for you as well Tristan." "Who are you?" Tristan asked, breathing heavy. Silence stood between them for a few minutes. The man walked towards him slowly and stopped when he saw Tristan back away. "I'm not going to hurt you son, I'm your father. You just have to understand the nature of what is happening here." He reached through the fog and retrieved a coin. Tossing it in the air, Tristan watched as it landed on its edge and spun. When it came to a stop it balanced on its ridge, heads facing him, looking at him with a stale face, "Pick it up. It's yours." He just looked at it and then back up at the man. "Pick it up!" the stranger yelled. Tristan shook startled and quickly bent down scooping up the coin and closing it in his fist. "I'm sorry Tristan but you, like the others, have a hard time listening and this why we are all in this situation right now." "Contrary to belief son, no one wants to hurt anyone. They just want to return to their loved ones. To be with the people that centuries have left behind." Tristan inched towards the door as the stranger paced back and forth near the window, looking out every so often at the tree and giving a soft smile not paying too much attention on Tristan's stance. "That is where you come in," he continued. "They seemed to have lost their payment to get to the others Tristan and you and your mommy are going to help me, them, us." He looked up at Tristan, as he froze solid in his tracks staring at the man. He continued to his pacing as he looked back out the window, "We tried to convince you and your family to listen but you just seemed to lack the ability to give us another way out." "We tried to use your dad as payment but the ferry man wanted nothing to do with such a weak and tired soul." "But," he turned to Tristan and smiled a huge grimace. "He did say that you and your mother would get most of them across. Now how could we turn that down?" Tristan dropped the coin and bolted for the door, "Pick up that coin boy!" The man screamed. Plaster and paint fell from the walls onto Tristan as he made his way down the stairs and out into the living room. The entire house shook and he could hear the wind grown as it tried to penetrate the house. A light appeared at the top of the stairs and he could see the feet of the stranger hover just above the ledge. Tristan took a deep breath and ran for the front door and just as he opened the door the man's voice boomed from behind him, "We have your mother Tristan and the tree will devour her unless you listen." Tristan stopped and turned towards the stranger floating down the stairwell. His face was contorted and grotesque, blood seeping from his nostrils and his gums clenched as trickles of saliva spider webbed down his chin to his collar. "She will not live another second Tristan and like your father it will be your fault." Tristan turned his head towards the open doorway and then quickly looked back at the stranger and stared for a few seconds, "Who are you?" It surprised the stranger, as he stood speechless. His teeth unclenched and his grimace fell a little. "If I come to you," the boy said. "Then tell me what you are and what they are." The man slowly descended the rest of the way down the staircase and then sat on the bottom step, pushing the plaster aside. "Well," he looked around. "This is but a surprise Tristan. You are willing to come to me but before you do you will trust me with what I am about to tell you?" Tristan shook his head yes and looked him straight in the eye. "If you lie, they will know and I think they won't take kindly to you if you lied to me." The stranger brushed his knees and looked at the floor. Tristan continued, "You refer to them as "they" like you are not part of them. Do you work for them? Why do you look like my dad? What do you really look like?" The man looked up at Tristan and smiled to the side of his mouth. "Alright son, I believe that it won't matter what you know in the end so I'll give you an explanation". Tristan inched towards the door a little more. You have no need to know who I am, just that I control who goes across the fields and who stays. The river man will take no one from the fields that have not the payment." The man looked up at Tristan and back to the floor. You had a gift Tristan, since the day you were born it seems. They noticed you the day you and your family came here. Your mother however? She hated the tree Tristan and the tree holds the souls of the lost here. The man who hung them from its branches confined them to the tree and so they wander the fields waiting. They have no payment for the ferryman and they have no way to get away from the tree. But you, you have a way, a gift. You could see the fields for what they really were Tristan. You could bring the masses across the fields letting the tree rest and so them." Tristan stopped inching and listened. "See son, you could get the ferry man to take payment from you, the coins. Then they could go, but your parents, the people. They just wouldn't listen no matter how many signs we had left." Tristan looked him in the eyes and walked to the doorway, "You lie." And he ran headed for the driveway. The stranger jumped from the stairs as Tristan slammed the door behind him. The man screamed from inside, "Your mothers flesh will be eaten by the worms boy! You will not escape them, no one escapes them!" Tristan ran off down the driveway and did not stop until he was in the main road. He breathed heavy as he looked back at the house and watched as dust and smoke bellowed from its walls. The foundation shook and the wind howled ripping at the siding. He would have to go back to find his mother. Tristan knew that the stranger didn't lie when he said they had her and what he would do to her. Tristan had to find a way to get them to let her go when he had no coins, nothing. He realized he still had no idea where she was and now he was alone. When John pulled onto the road leading to the house he could see the dust rising from the house walls, bellowing into the air. He slammed on the breaks and searched for his cell phone, finding it and realizing it was dead, no power at all, *what the hell?* He set it on his passenger seat and proceeded slowly towards the house. He soon realized that it wasn't a fire. Tristan was standing in the middle of the road at the end of the driveway and he pulled up closer, stopped the car and got out when Tristan looked at him and began to walk his way cautiously. John waved his hands at Tristan, "I'm a friend of your mom and dad's. I'm from your dads firm, I'm John Stathom." Tristan got within five feet of him and stopped looked back at the house and then stared back at John. "Are you okay son?" Tristan just looked at the house again and then turned to him, "You don't want to go to that house. My mom and dad are gone and they want me." "Tristan," John walked up next to him, "where are your parents?" He looked at the car and then to the ground. "My dad is, dead and my mom is somewhere in the house I think, but they are there and they want me to go back or they will kill my mother." John bent down, "Who are they Tristan, did you call the cops, and does anyone know what is going on?" The boy shook his head and looked back at the house. Dust flew from the windows and the wind carried it towards its sides. "What is that coming from out of the house Tristan, fire?" Tristan shrugged and looked at John, "I think so. It was there when I got back from the field." "What were you doing in the field?" John looked puzzled. Staring wide-eyed at the house, Tristan shrugged his shoulders again, "They had brought me out there where they had killed my father and when I came to the house looking for my mother, they had sent someone to get me." "Who are they Tristan? Listen you need to get into my car and we will go get someone to help." Without hesitation Tristan began to walk away from John and towards the house, "They won't stop until I find them and help them." He turned towards John stopping, "You can come with me if you want to help, but you don't have to." Without another word, he turned and began to walk back towards the driveway again. John went back to his car and grabbed his phone from his seat along with his keys, "Wait Tristan," he called ahead. Tristan just kept walking as John jogged to catch him. It was dark and wet and she felt like someone had beaten her. Her legs felt broken and her spine was numb. When she opened her eyes slightly, all she could see was the ground, dirt and grass. The sky was hazy and the smell of dead leaves filled her nostrils and mouth. Jody knew she was near the tree but she wasn't sure where, exactly. Her head pounded and the taste of stale blood filled her throat. Suddenly she was aware of how close to the tree she was when the groan of its movement filled the air above her. Jody lifted herself to her knees and looked up at its trunk as it twisted and bent as though it were human. The house was releasing dust clouds from its windows and siding as the roof puffed, throwing shingles onto the yard and was slowly being torn from its foundation. Out from the back door she watched as the stranger that looked like her husband walked into the yard and stared out towards the field. Jody knew that the field was the key and the destruction of the field will be the destruction of them. The stranger looked over at her and gave a Cheshire grin, "Oh Jody, I see that you have come to. How do you like your home?" He turned and smirked at his work. "They will not wait any longer and they have the boy. Like his father, he will be sacrificed so they may move on." He walked to the edge of the yard and the tree bent and touched his feet. The stranger looked out the corner of his eye, "I do not need you anymore Jody and I shall have to get rid of you. Like so many before you they decided you shall hang from the tree and there you shall stay until we can pay your way through the fields." She stood up, legs shaking and tried to walk away from the tree and towards the house. The tree turned to her and wrapped a branch around her neck. She could feel it tightening, taking her breath. Jody twitched and tried to pull the branch free but it began to lift her to her toes, teasing her. Her head began to swim and the back of her eyes felt as if they would burst from her skull. The stranger looked over only once to admire her demise and then looked back out into the ocean of grass. Putting his hands outward the grass bent towards him and his smile widened, showing his teeth. Jody began to fade, her breath was getting harder and harder to achieve and then she closed her eyes and let the branch crush her throat. She could remember Tristan and Dustin as they were. Tristan when he was a baby, the day she and Dustin married and when they bought the house. Now the very same tree she wanted to destroy has turned its vengeance on her. The last thing she could remember seeing was the stranger smiling towards the field as the grass reached for him, caressing his feet. What of Tristan? What would they do to him? She could do nothing now, just die. *I love you Tristan.* The stranger stood on the edge of the field and pointed his nose to the air. The smell of burnt grass and dirt spilled into the back of his throat and consumed him with joy. The smile on his face split across his cracked cheeks making his already contorted face seem madder. The fog around his body danced and caressed his waist, shoulders and legs, loving him, nurturing him, pleasing the stranger and making him aware of its presence to succumb to his will. The horizon separated the field from the sky with a pinkish hue. The grass in the distance leaned away from it as if it wished not to converse with its beauty. His eyes flashed light out from behind them and into the distance, beyond the silhouettes of a thousand beings stood affixed like dead trees in the field, awaiting the obvious. The tree would lean and beckon for the grass to touch its leaves and show its alliance. The stranger ignored the dance and held his arms out to the silhouettes, "Soon my loved ones, we will have the boy and then, then the ferryman will let us go beyond the fields, beyond the pain of this retched farmer's hell that we have called home for years!" The horizon splashed colors in response as the night began to take over and the distant watchers faded with the afternoon sky. "They will listen! He continued, "They will bring us to the glory land." He turned to see the tree display sadness as the grass grew darker and darker and the night began its rise to power. He looked back at the house and lowered his hands. His head twisted in an inhuman way his cheek touching his left shoulder. He opened his mouth exposing his teeth to the night air and screeched a loud hiss that sent distant animal's scurrying into the night for safer refuge. The house shook and the tree stood silent as the stranger regained his posture and ran his hands down the side of his coat. In the distance the echo of his mad screech disappeared into the horizon scaring off the remainder of the day, "Tristan!" he called out. The driveway seemed as good as place as any for them to sit for awhile and figure out what they were going to do. When the loud noise filled the air from the back of the house they had stopped in their tracks and stood staring at the house in amazement, "What the hell was that?" John looked down at Tristan. "It's them sir. They are coming and I have no idea how many of them there are." John's eyes widened, "How many do you think?" The boy looked up and nodded. "I've only heard them in my mind but I know there must be a lot of them." Tristan had explained some of what was going on when they began the slow walk towards the house. John hadn't believed much of it and actually thought the boy was a bit loony. His stance on the subject took a slight turn when they had heard that screeching noise from out back of the house. "What are these, they, whatever you call them?" Tristan looked to the night, "Not sure really. I thought they were aliens at first but now. Not sure." John had realized that he had left his smokes on the front seat of his car and gave out a sigh. "Well", he looked back at the road now quite far away. "What are we going to do Tristan?" The boy shrugged. "My mom is there somewhere sir, I can't leave her here. They will kill her, like daddy." The sky had now turned dark blue and purple, the stars were barely making a scene and John got a slight cold chill. Tristan just stood there silent, staring at the house. He wasn't sure where the stranger was and what he would do when he found him. He had his mother and he wanted Tristan. Tristan had to figure out what he wanted with them and had not heard one single voice in quite some time, feeling they may have entirely left his body. They didn't need him to listen or to make others listen anymore so what did they want him to do now? Maybe it was over, his mother dead and the stranger gone with "them". It was quite and the house had finally rested, sleeping for the night it seemed. John looked down at Tristan for a sign on what to do and then looked back towards his car regretting leaving his cigarettes. It was too dark to see it clearly and that made him nervous when he thought he might not be able to find it if he had to run.

CHAPTER 6

The house seemed quiet. This was the way he liked it when he playing alone. His figures were poised just right on the hard wood floor and the battle field was prepared. He could hear his mother downstairs getting laundry and saying a few curse words here and there. Dad was out in the back yard on one of his random days off doing the lawn. The smell of grass filled the living room and his mom and dad had nagged him to go out and play. One of those "get some sunshine" lines all kids hated when they were not in the mood to "get some sun." Looking back down upon the war at hand, the red solider stood upon the block wall and sized up the row of armed men awaiting him. He could take them and Tristan put him there because he never lost, it was his favorite soldier. There were many others that he liked but nothing like the red one. Even in the movies and the comics, this was it. This was the man of the hour. He reached for the figure and just as his fingers grasped it, there was a tingle that filled his head. It was a tingle that he was learning to get used and he knew they were knocking. His mother marched up the stairs and paused at the door jam, "Tristan honey, you hungry?" He couldn't answer and his muscled tensed in his neck, his head began to shake back and forth. "Let me know then ok?" and she whistled away into the kitchen sitting the clothes on the table. Tristan could feel them enter his head and this was something that he hated the most when they came. He never heard the voices at first, it was always the tingle and then they would take over his body. When he was just a small child they whispered sweetly to him but now they controlled him, talked to him harshly, answered questions without his consent. He was hungry but they had a different agenda for now. He stood up slowly and was walked to the basement door. As they turned his head to see where Jody was, he slipped into the stairwell and made his way down to the cold floor. Still wearing his pajamas and socks, he wished he had gotten dressed when his dad hounded him at breakfast. The room was dark and Tristan could hear the washer filling. They turned his head, searching the room and he found himself just staring into the darkness of the basement hoping they would leave him soon. He was lead into the dark corner of the room and there against the wall a dark figure swayed back and forth. It didn't seem human but had somewhat of a human form. Tristan began to panic but there nothing he could do. He felt his throat open to scream but they had stopped him before anything could escape into the cold basement air. The figure seemed to calm its sway, as Tristan got closer, staring with shiny glass like eyes. Tristan's mouth opened and a strange serious of sounds came out; clicks and snaps filled his ears as the figure responded with a similar tone. Tristan began to breath heavy and tried to fight what was happening. They conversed back and forth and Tristan got a better look at the figure when it got closer. Its head was short and stubby and its eyes were normal sized but glossy, black and deep. It looked human but deformed, like a monster from one of those movies his dad always watched, *the boogeyman?* All of the sudden the lights burst on and they let Tristan drop to the floor with his chest heaving. Jody ran to him and bent down looking at him in shock, "Are you ok? What were you doing down here Tristan, you know you are not allowed to be down here honey?" Her voice was filled with worry and anger as Tristan looked up in a panic for the monster in the corner. It was gone and the corner looked peaceful and normal in the light. Tristan breathed heavy and grappled his mothers arm trying to get up and run. Jody lifted him to his feet and walked him upstairs. His dad rushed in and began to call the doctors as he walked back and forth with a worried look, "What was it Tristan, a seizure?" his dad asked holding his palm over the receiver. Jody went to the sink and got Tristan some water. Bringing it to him she stopped and looked down at Tristan's hand, "Where did you get the coin honey?" Tristan's first visit to the doctors that summer was like all others. He didn't want to be there and it was a long wait with his mom and dad pacing the floor while he watched cartoons in the waiting room. Nurses would come out and look around as if they knew someone, glance at a clipboard and then try her best shot at some foreign name or nail the easy ones right on the nose, like "Smith? Tanya Smith?" Tristan seemed to ignore the hours that passed and would occasionally look up at his parents to make sure they were still there. When he was finally called, Jody and Dustin would smile and scoop Tristan up like they only had a second to decide before someone else's name was called. The hall ways were always empty at that hospital and the doors to the rooms were always shut. If one door was opened it was either empty or it was opened just a crack so you couldn't truly see inside. Tristan would twist his neck in attempt to look into the crack and see what horrible thing they were keeping secret. Most likely it was a mangled body or an old decayed man that held out his hand and moaned in pain. Tristan remembered seeing things like that when he would sneak into the living room to see what movie his dad was watching. He was never caught and only stayed a few minutes which was mostly spent covering his eyes. Dustin would smile at Tristan's faces as they passed the rooms, Jody just walked like it was death row. She hated the hospitals and knew it would end the same way, no answers. It was always "Well, the tests are fine and your son seems normal Mrs. Burns." Sometimes they would come up with some strange condition and then prompt them to see a specialist which in turn ended with a nice loop to the hospital again. She just wanted answers. The seizures were getting worse and Tristan was beginning to act stranger and stranger. Always needing to carry quarters, speaking about his friends and how no one would listen to them. "What friends honey, listen to what?" He never had an answer and it made her think that maybe he didn't know himself, maybe he was going crazy. Not her son. She couldn't bear the thought of her baby being sent to some children's hospital to be held in a cold room and drugged, forgotten. Not her son. When they had been in the room for an hour or so Tristan would find his toys in his mom's purse and try to set up a battle of some type. The white covered beds never really made a good field, there was nowhere to hide. Dustin would watch and once in a while ask Tristan what the battle was for this time? Tristan broke into character every time and began to throw terms that Dustin only pretended to understand. That would always take a good twenty minutes, giving the doctor plenty of time to walk in, put down his things and stare as they do. But this time it was a bit different. The doctor walked in, interrupted Tristan and Dustin and asked if the nurse may take Tristan to get some stickers up front for a moment. Jody began to breath heavy and Tristan hopped off the bed and went happily with the nurse, leaving his battle at a stalemate once more. No sooner did the door close when the doctor leaned up against the sink area and looked Dustin up and down, "Your boy has a situation Mr. and Mrs. Burns. It seems that a CAT scan shows some damage to his frontal lobe." He picked up an envelope from his stack of things. This is some other tests that we ran, blood test mostly, but we have no explanation for what we saw next." Jody went over to Dustin and held his shoulder, squeezing it. The doctor retrieved a large white envelope and pulled out to X-rays. Putting them up to the light he signaled them both to come and look. They weren't sure what they were looking for but the doctor used his pen to show them the area of question. "This is a crack in the front part of his skull, from some trauma not reported by either one of you. Why?" They looked at the doctor dumbfounded, "I didn't know Tristan had such an injury doctor." Dustin stared at him amazed. The doctor looked at Jody and then held up the second one. "Well, no bother Mr. Burns, when we took the second shot two minutes later," he paused and out lined his subject of interest again, "Gone." He said calmly. Dustin and Jody stepped back and stared at the doctor. Putting down the x-rays he leaned up against the counter again and fixed his jacket. "It seems that right after this last x-ray was taken, Tristan went into some type of seizure. They had to hold him down on the table when he tried to get up. Kept yelling something about how "they need to listen", whose they?" Jody covered her mouth and sat on the bed, "We don't know sir," Dustin walked over to Jody. "Tristan said this the first time he had an episode and we keep asking him who, but he doesn't say. How did he get that, crack? How did it heal within seconds?" The doctor stood up straight and grabbed his things from the counter. He slowly opened the door and looked at Jody, "I don't know Mr. and Mrs. Burns, it's been reported and there some people coming here within the hour to see your son. Seems they have an interest in this case, a high interest. Tristan will be right back, okay" Dustin shook his head in agreement and as soon as the door shut he gathered Tristan's things and looked around the room. "What are you doing?" Jody said on the verge of tears. "They will take Tristan from us Jody and we will never see him again. What happened here is not normal and they never said anything about calling anyone before." She stood up and got her purse. The nurse knocked on the door and Tristan burst in all smiles with a handful of stickers. "Look mom! They gave me cool glow in the dark stickers and," "That's good honey." She said and put her arm around his shoulder. When the nurse left Dustin looked out the door and when he caught the chance they walked out into the lobby and rushed to his car. Tristan didn't think anything of it and as they pulled away from the drive they could see three men in suits get out of a van labeled "Department of Medical Development" and flash they're badges at a doctor waiting outside. Just before he went out to the main street, the four men looked at them as the doctor pointed and was shaking his head. The last night Tristan could remember having a real life was the night he saw the figure from the basement for the last time. After dinner they had decided that movie night was the best idea and settled down with a huge bowl of popcorn and iced tea. Tristan could remember being carried up the stairs by his mom or dad, he wasn't sure which. When he woke up the moon light had made the room a bluish hue that made him feel like he was in some kind of fantasy world. He looked over at his Darth Vader alarm clock and sighed when he read three thirty. The air was cold and he could feel a light breeze over his nose. He sat up and looked over towards his window and noticed the curtains dancing. *Who opened my window, jeez?* Putting his feet to the even colder floor he shivered for a second then stood up and studied the room for a minute. He was never really one to be scared of the dark and the room didn't bother him a bit. Sometimes he would get up and wander the house because he thought it looked cool at night time. It was always different when his dad was watching one of those scary movies or telling mom about one. They never seemed to show what it was really like at night time, at least what it was like for Tristan, it was peace and quiet. When he approached the window he could feel the breeze take a hold of him and it made him shake. It was always like this no matter what season and it was death in the winter.

"You wouldn't want to even get near a window in these parts during winter." The night sky was crystal clear and he looked out into the back yard and into the field. It swayed with the wind like a giant sea filled with secrets and hidden creatures to guard them. He never went into the field as long as they had lived there and his dad and mom would kill him if they ever found out differently. They were over afraid of what might happen. Did a hunter leave a trap out there or are there snakes or spiders? Tristan always laughed it off and just played in the back yard and dreamed about what might be out in that sea. Every so often he could see some grass move out of place and then some strange sounds come from the distance, Raccoons *probably*. The yard looked pretty still and the big tree loomed over the edge into the field like a protector. He wanted to climb that beast but his mother made sure that wasn't going to happen. She locked every ladder and climbing utensil they had in the basement and told him how much she hated that tree and soon, it would be chopped down. He couldn't understand why she didn't like it; it's just a tree. There it stood and she would never get that thing down, no one could. Tristan walked to his bedroom door and peaked out to listen for his dads snoring. He had been caught out in the house a couple of times and was grounded for a week. So now, his nighttime wanders will be planned before attempting. As soon as he heard the grumble he knew all was safe and nothing was going to wake that monster. He stepped into the hallway and looked both ways as he crept to the bathroom. He entered and didn't even turn on the light. He knew where the toilet was by heart and could use it with a blind fold on. He would always wonder if he was a super human. How many other people could walk around the house in the dark and never bump into anything, let alone use the bathroom without any sight at all, *Super human*. He reached down and pulled up the seat and in the dark proceeded to do his business. A smile curled his lips as he heard the water and not the rim being hit, *Super human*. There was a loud thud from somewhere in the house and Tristan froze silent. All he could hear was liquid hitting liquid. When that stopped he didn't even breathe. That would wake the beast for sure and it was really loud, he had to of heard that. Several minutes passed until he relaxed a little and pulled up his pants. He was waiting for his dad or mom to burst into the bathroom where there he at least had an alibi. If he stepped one foot into the hallway and was caught then, it was over.

Even if it looked as though he was returning from the bathroom they wouldn't take his word for it, grounded. When he took the first couple steps into the hallway, he made sure that it was silent. *What the heck was that?* The sound came from downstairs somewhere, at least that he was sure of. But what it came from was a different thing all together. Did a cat get into the house or some other animal? When he passed his parents room it was on tippy toes. That was ground zero and there was no way he was getting nailed there. As a matter of fact as long as he was out of his room, not in the bathroom or in their room, it was ground zero. The door to their lair was shut and he passed without incident. When he looked down the stairs it was double panic. First he had to listen for whatever it was that made that sound as well as his parents getting up and catching him wandering again. Each step was judged with caution. The house was old and made sounds that would surprise anyone. Every board had its own creak. Every door had its own slam. From outside the house looked well put together but from the inside, although well decorated, it was well dated. When he reached far enough down to see into the living room a little he scoped the surroundings. Everything seemed still and he paused for a bit more, one for his parents and one for his nerves. When he stepped onto the floor at the bottom of the stairs he looked out into the living room and then into the kitchen, the living room looked empty and he walked slowly to the entrance keeping and extra eye in the other direction. The darkness seemed thicker when he was closer and now his assumption was under scrutiny. Scanning the room he walked to the center and stood waiting for a sound, something. A cold chill ran down his spine and he turned his head to the side and saw a shadow of something in the entry way five feet behind him. He turned around slowly and looked directly at a figure swaying back and forth. Tristan froze when he realized what it was. "What do you want?" The figure just stood there looking at him with shiny black eyes. It moved slowly towards him and Tristan went to scream and yet he didn't. The figure put his hand in the air and began to click and snap vocally. At first Tristan tried to understand and he watched it move and look at him. He knew it wasn't here to harm him and watched as it continued to click and snap, pointing to the ceiling, looking around and then back at Tristan with glossy eyes. Tristan became concerned when he realized how loud the figure was being. He took a step forward and it straightened its posture and looked down at him from a seven-foot stretch. Tristan stepped back and put his hands up. Before he could do anything, the figure turned and ran to the kitchen. Tristan paused, and then took off after it. The back door was open and he could hear it on the back porch stomping around. A light flashed at the top of the stairs and Tristan could see another figure coming down to investigate. The figure took one look at the door and went out into the night. He stood on the west end of the porch and looked directly at Tristan then to the field. Tristan took one step towards it and the figure held up its hand above his head, jumped onto the grass and stopped. It looked at the field and then at Tristan, and before he could do anything the figure spoke to him. In a crackly, gargling human like voice it turned his head, "listen" it said and then took off into the field so fast Tristan barely had time to jump off the porch and head for the edge of the yard. As he stood there, he heard his father yell for him from the porch door. He turned around and could tell there was no way to explain this and his father did not looked pleased, even from this far away. The travel to the porch was like a death row walk and his dad just looked down at him as he passed him into the kitchen. "You know you're gonna be grounded for a long time right?" Tristan just nodded and headed for his room. When he heard his dad snoring again he went to his window and opened it as far as it could. The field just swayed as it did earlier and Tristan knew that the thing from the basement was out there watching him from the sea of grass. Listen it said, like the voices in his head. Why did the voices not come tonight? Whatever that thing was it understood him and had a message like the voices. Is this were the voices come from? Do they look like it? He waited all night and for several months he waited every night. It never returned and Tristan never saw the figure again. The hospital corridor was bare with the scent of cleaner and sickness. The three men waited for the doctors. Two skinny men walked into the room holding clipboards and badges. One of the officers stepped forward, "My name is Officer Mitchelle." He looked to his side and gestured, "This is Officer Kent and Officer Brunnel. Do you have information and are they where they cannot leave the building?" Both doctors nodded and extended their hands only to be ignored by the three suits. They looked to the ground for a second and handed the clipboards over to Officer Mitchelle. The three men turned away and looked around for a place to sit. "Do you have a private room so that we may evaluate these documents?" They were led down the hallway to an office and before the two doctors could explain where they were they were told to wait until they came out. The look on their faces told the two young doctors that they were not asking. The room was dim and it seemed like an office that was barely used if at all. They went to a desk that was rummaged with notepads, papers and an old computer that may be used for more of a paperweight. On the edge of the desk there was a picture of the one doctor and his two kids. They were an attractive family but the kids could use some braces. Mitchelle cleaned off a section of the desk and made himself as comfortable as he could in the doctor's chair. The clipboard had a brief history about Tristan and the reason for his visit today. Brunnel flipped through the other clipboard and was examining some charts when he came across a slip. Handing it to Mitchelle he looked back to his clipboard. The slip was a note from a doctor months before. It seems that Tristan's blood work needed to be re-examined do to a very high level of Triglycerides. He thumbed through his clipboard and then signaled for Brunnel's. After a good fifteen minutes of searching he came across a chart that showed the blood work mentioned on the slip. The Triglyceride levels were a staggering four thousand seven hundred and ten. There was number count on the right side that read the levels before, one hundred and five. There was special notation on the side "???? Re-check ASAP????" Mitchelle piled the two clipboards on top of each other. "Get those two in here so we can find out what they know." Kent opened the door and signaled them in. Standing in his office the doctor scanned to see if anything was moved or gone through. Mitchelle looked at them and sat quietly for a second. "Why are they here today and for what were we called for?" One doctor looked over and pointed to the chart. "It says on the back there that if this patient comes here to notify you immediately sir." Mitchelle remembered sending that note to every hospital back when they got away the first time. "What do you or this hospital know about this young boy?" "Well", the other spoke up. "He has been here in the past and he has a history of seizure activity. He had an incident at a fast food parking lot today and that's all that we were aware of thus far. You were notified before we ran any special tests or continued further." Brunnel walked over and scooped up the top clipboard. "So," he looked at the chart.

"Does he exhibit any odd behavior or anything that would lead you to believe that he is different than your common patient?" "As I said before sir, we have done nothing to come to that conclusion. You were to be notified before we proceeded with any testing out of the normal blood tests and exam." Mitchelle stood up and retrieved the clipboard from Brunnel and handed both of them to the doctor nearest the door. "We need to see the child. You need to make sure that they are secure and are unable to leave until we speak to them." The doctors opened the door and entered the hallway. Mitchelle pulled out his wallet and brandished business cards, handing them to each of them. "If you hear anything when we leave today you be sure to call me right away." The doctors pocketed the cards and turned leading them down a turn and into a long hallway that was empty of any patients. It seemed that this entire wing seemed to be vacant and used for other purposes than patient care. The door to the room was shut and they could hear the mother in there talking to herself. Mitchelle looked at the two doctors and the other men. "No matter what is said we are here to investigate her as a concern from the state. Think of it as child abuse concern." The two doctors looked at each other and knew that this was far from the case but had no choice but to do as instructed. Mitchelle then went into some false conversation about a bar tab and opened the door. "Hello Mrs. Burns, we just have a few questions to ask you and then these two doctors have a few as well, ok." When John Stathom received the call from Officer Mitchelle it came as no surprise that there was going to be some bullshitting here and there. The information would come easy and the truth would probably be wilder then the lies, they usually were. They decided it was best to meet and have a conference of sorts to discuss information on both sides. Mitchelle had made John aware of the circumstances at hand and that he and his company were in a situation that wasn't to be handled lightly. John didn't like to hear that and understood that the word "lawsuit" could be thrown out there. It was his job to hush that term and bury it with as much dirt as he could. The problem with this was that the Department of Medical Development had no dirt and the history was clouded and protected by bulldog lawyers that made John look like a Boy Scout troop leader. The meeting was not an option and John made sure to watch his tone and pay close attention to this Mitchelle character, something on both sides of this story has issues and it was in his best interest to find out just exactly what the hell that was. The drive to the meeting was spent going over what questions he would ask and what he would make sure he would avoid. What did they want with this kid in the first place? The company would John responsible for anything that went wrong with this situation and if it was in the best interest of the company, he would have to drop Dustin. He searched for his phone along with a cigarette and found the phone first. As he attempted to drive, dial and find his cigarettes he soon realized that smoking wasn't the only thing could kill him at this point. He held the phone to his ear and immediately got Dustin's cell phone message. As soon as he heard the beep, "Yeah, Dustin, you need to give me a call as soon as you get this ok. I have a few questions and I have some answers to the questions about this company." He had yet to acquire any information but by the time Dustin called him back he would have gained a little. Dustin has been notorious so far in taking his sweet time getting back to him. He decided that pulling over to get a cigarette was in his best interest as well and yanked his steering wheel to the right as he closed and dropped his phone on the passenger seat. His soft pack was a bit tattered and only held one or two left. He sighed as he fished one out and fumbled for his lighter in his pocket. As he lit his smoke and cracked the window the cell phone rang. It was his wife. He smiled at the phone and pulled out into the road. The sky was looking a little dim and the clouds were beginning to blacken. John hated rainy days and on the way to a meeting with a stranger he knew he wouldn't care for just made the migraine feeling build. When he pulled up to the café he looked around for this Mitchelle guy as if he was going to be able to spot him from every other suit in the place. He sat in his car and checked his phone to see if Dustin called and shoved it in his pocket with a disappointed look. He got out and did one last scan as he began to walk to the entrance. When he entered the air was filled with cappuccino and latte with ginger and some other fragrance that reminded him why he sent his secretary to get him his coffee fix. Over in the far corner stood a man in a tight dark suit, he looked directly at John and waved him over. *Does this guy know me?* As he strolled over he could tell by the look on this man's face that he didn't like the place any more than he did. "Would you like a coffee Mr. Stathom?" John shook his head no, "You can call me John." The man smiled. "You can call me Office Mitchelle." John didn't return the smile and looked for a table to sit at. Mitchelle followed him across the room into a corner and sat down as far from others as they could get, which was not an easy order. The place was packed with what seemed like every person in the county. John couldn't help but think why this individual picked this place in the first place. He didn't strike him as a dumb man so the only thing that sat in his mind is that Mitchelle wanted people around for some reason or another. "So," John looked him up and down. "What's this all about?" The man got himself comfortable and reached into his jacket pocket. He pulled out a folded paper and ever so carefully opened it and handed it to John. He studied John's reaction and then began to chime in. That is the figure we are offering you to help us find out what they are hiding at the home. John looked at Mitchelle and then back down at the paper. "And what is it that you think they are doing?" Mitchelle didn't give a quick answer, instead he pointed to the paper, "that's why we are willing to pay you. The parents wouldn't let us within five feet of the home and we have been watching this boy for a long time, John." It didn't make a hell of a lot of sense and John and he chose his words wisely. "What is it that you guys want for me to do? Get info, or do you want me to get them to let you in?" The officer mad a stern face and then rubbed his pant leg studying John. "The boy has been exhibiting some behavior that the government finds interesting and they would like to evaluate the boy." Now John sat up to attention and understood why the man acted the way he did. "Something illegal I take it?" Mitchelle looked around for a second and shook his head no. "The Environmental and Space Exploratory has a big interest and that is who I work for. They lead the forefront on stellar communication and also in some cases the supernatural." John was in disbelief to what he was hearing and he smiled at Mitchelle, waiting for him to start laughing and his friends jumping out, big joke. But as he sat there he realized that Mitchelle was dead serious and he looked back down at the paper and realized the figure was no joke either. "What is this all about, if I'm in then I'm in." Mitchelle cut him off right there and let him know who decided what. "Well I'm sorry but that isn't an option. You can take the money and do what we need with no questions as to why. Or you can walk away." John knew that this wasn't really that cut and dry. If he didn't take the money then he probably wouldn't make it home. "What is it you need me to do?" Mitchelle, for the first time relaxed and extended his hand to John. This didn't make John feel any more at ease and he knew that he made a deal that not even the devil would take. "All they need is for you to go to the house and investigate what is going on. Make sure you play it out because if anyone thinks for one second that you are going for any other purpose, there could be a problem." John knew he meant that he just needed to keep his mouth shut and get the info they needed. Then if he felt, with this money, he could retire for three years. "Ok," he smiled. "What are you guys looking for exactly?" Mitchelle leaned in slowly and put his hand on John's knee, "The boy. Get the boy." When Dustin entered the field after Tristan his heart leapt from his chest. His son was acting so strangely and Dustin knew this wasn't some seizure. He could hear Jody yelling and then silence. He looked back only once and saw her lying there. He turned back for a second and then turned to see Tristan continue through the grass. He bent down and took a deep breath. Then turned toward Tristan and headed in to the grass after him. "Tristan!" he yelled but the boy just kept moving. He seemed to float through the field as if the grass carried him like a god. Dustin could barely keep up with him and had to stop and catch his breath. The sky was getting lower it seemed and the Tristan kept getting further away every time he stopped. "Tristan, damn it!" he shouted. The boy didn't listen as if in a trance he kept floating into the field. Dustin looked back at the house and then realized that he was too far in to see Jody anymore. When he spun back to see how far Tristan was, the boy was gone from sight. He began to panic and looked around the horizon to see if maybe he might have headed for the far left or right, nothing. Tristan was nowhere to be seen and Dustin realized that he was also far out into the field and alone. As he turned to head back for the house he felt a tingle in his spine and then a sudden swoosh of pain shook his entire body. He dropped to the ground and curled in a ball. The pain was like fire shooting from his head to his feet and his eyes felt as if they would pop from the socket. Putting his hands on his head he screamed and called for Tristan. The pain suddenly stopped, and as he breathed, he opened his eyes and saw feet about three feet from his face. He looked up and saw Tristan staring down at him with a plain look across his face, "Tristan, where did you go son?" Dustin crawled to his knees and sat up slowly. As he looked into his boys eyes he could tell that what he was looking at was not Tristan. Something that looked like his boy was staring down at him with a strange Cheshire grin. "Who are you?" The stranger turned his head to the side and then let out this retched screech that made Dustin throw his hands to his ears and bow his head. When the sound ceased, Dustin looked back up and held his hand up to touch the stranger. With a fast grab Dustin's hand was twisted completely backwards and the bone snapped through the skin, blood squirting onto the strangers face. With his tongue he licked the side of his mouth and watched as Dustin's screams filled the field. The grass seemed to dance back and forth in joy of his pain and whatever had taken over Tristan was enjoying it as well. Picking up a stick from the side of his feet the stranger began to chop at the grass to make a clearing around Dustin. The grass didn't fight the onslaught and laid down for him with every strike. Dustin sat up and held his hand close to his body. "What are you doing? What have we done to you?" The thing just chopped at the grass and ignored the pleading. "Where is my son?" The stranger turned and ran up to Dustin and got up in his face so close Dustin could see his skin was more see-thru than actual skin. Standing straight up the stranger lifted the stick and with no hesitation began to beat Dustin over the head repeatedly. Screeches filled the air and the field went silent. Back at the house the sound was barely audible, but the tree danced in the wind as if it carried the news to it so they could both rejoice. Jody lay quite and the day crept away leaving the field to the dim horizon. Dustin lay there in a lump, and the stranger bent down to look at its work. He leaned over the body and then put its hand on Dustin's bloody shoulder. Shaking, its flesh began to peel away and light shot out from its back and neck. The meat fell away and a fog began to surround the figure. When it stood again the fog hugged its body and Dustin's face held a grimace smirk where Tristan's face one was. The figure looked to the horizon and dropped the stick, "Tristan!" It called out with Dustin's voice and the grass bent down to its mercy.

CHAPTER 7

Brunnel, Kent and Mitchelle sat in the hotel room just outside of town. They knew that John might be a risk and they may need to do the job themselves. John was expendable and from what they were told, at this point, so were the boy's parents. They were told that getting the boy was the prime objective. In the years that Mitchelle had worked for the company they had never been this strict and forceful with a job. This child must have something amazing. None of them knew exactly what the boy had or could do, but whatever it was the company would do what was needed to get him and this was where they were. It had been several hours since John had called and said he was on his way there, Kent began to question John's loyalty and Mitchelle quickly shut him up. "Give the man some time Kent. We have no idea what is going on at the moment." Kent walked to the bathroom and looked in the mirror, judging his shadow to see if it was time to shave. "Well if he doesn't call soon Mitchelle then we need to call and find out what they want us to do, at least how long we should wait." Mitchelle understood where Kent was coming from, and the company let them know days ago just how important this was. It would all fall back on them if this whole thing went down badly or the boy was not in their possession. Mitchelle wondered what they needed this boy so badly for, but he kept that question to himself. He knew it was wise to never make the team question the mission and it would lead to questions about what they were doing. "If we do not hear from Mr. Stathom within the hour we will take it upon ourselves to go to the house." Kent and Brunnel shook their heads in agreement and Kent went back to examine his face. Brunnel fished through channels and made himself comfortable on the hard bed while Mitchelle got up and headed for the door. "I'm gonna take a walk, let me know if ya hear anything all right?" He walked out of the room, not waiting for a response, entering the parking lot with a sigh. He felt the pressure of the whole mission and began to question John himself. What if he told the family and they were on their way to safety? He thought about the face John made when he opened the paper at the café. He was sure that he wouldn't be a problem and until Kent's outburst he wasn't worried at all. The hotel was pretty much vacant and only one or two lights shown from draped windows. He felt like he was in a scene from psycho. He couldn't wait until this whole thing was done with. He hadn't told Brunnel and Kent that he didn't even have orders as of what to do when they had the boy. What about John? Was he just supposed to let him walk away and say "Thank you for your service"? There were a lot of holes to fill in and he needed to find out what was next. He fished for his phone and called his leading officer. The phone rang only once and a stern voice answered. "Sir, I'm sorry to bother you. We haven't heard from Mr. Stathom yet and I was wondering the next course of action?" He looked back at the hotel room door to make sure one of them didn't walk out. The voice on the other side requested the last time Mr. Stathom was spoken to? Mitchelle took a breath, "a couple of hours, sir." There was a slight pause and then he was told to sit tight and give Stathom another hour and then call him. Mitchelle took a deep breath and then let it spill. "What are we supposed to do with the boy and Mr. Stathom when they arrive?" "Get rid of Stathom and then call me when the boy is in your sole possession." Mitchelle heard a click and the line was dead. The night had a different feel than five minutes ago and he looked back at the room and put his phone back in his pocket. Walking up to the door he opened it slowly and crossed the room to the bathroom. Kent was sitting on the bed next to Brunnel laughing at some sitcom. Mitchelle shut the door and sat on the toilet and thought this thing over for a second. They were going to have to kill Stathom, do what with his body, who knew? Take the boy and drive somewhere and call his lead officer when the boy was in his sole possession, sole possession? It hit him that it meant that Brunnel and Kent would not be in the picture either. He didn't directly say that and yet he said sole possession. Mitchelle started to think that maybe he was looking to deep into this as he got up and paced the room for a second. He paused in front of the mirror and looked at himself. *Think Mitchelle, what the hell was going on? What were they gonna do? Would you even be spared in the secret ?*He could hear the two idiots laughing out there and it broke his concentration. He walked out into the room and noticed the door was still open, cold air filling the room. "Hey assholes, you plan on shutting the door?" He walked over and slammed it. Kent and Brunnel sat up and realized something wasn't right. "What's going on Mitchelle?" The officer turned to his colleagues, ran his fingers through his hair and leaned against the door. "I just got off the phone with the lead officer and he informed me that Stathom was to be hit and the boy brought to them when in my sole custody." They sat quietly and stared at Mitchelle. He could tell by the look in their faces that they knew what was meant. "Listen guys, I don t even think I'm going to walk away from this situation. It's safe to say that we need to understand that whatever the hell they want with this kid it is a lot bigger than any of us can comprehend." Kent got up and paced the room near the bed and looked at Brunnel. "We need to get to that house and get that kid. If we have him then we can find out what the company wants." Mitchelle shook his head and pointed at Kent. "No, that's not going to happen. They will come and hunt us down like dogs guys. We need to play by the rules and when we get the kid, drop him off and get the hell out and disappear." Brunnel liked that idea and shut off the television. He got up and walked towards Mitchelle, "that would be the way if what you say is true. Are you sure that he said it just like that or are you reading into things?" Kent just stared at the floor in thought as Mitchelle responded. "Well I am not going to take a chance and find out Brunnel. "If John is to be hit when he was paid then what's to say our money was ever meant to be dished out either, if we were so trusted then why haven't they once let us know exactly what was going on with this kid?" The others looked at each other and Kent chimed in. "Ok, let's get on our way towards the house and we will call John when we are closer and wait to see what he has for us." Mitchelle grabbed the hotel keys and went out the door towards the van. Kent and Brunnel returned the keys to the hotel and met Mitchelle at the end of the driveway. When they left the hotel they were very aware that the night was about to get strange and if they were lucky it would end with them on their way to Mexico with or without the money. The trip to the house was partly quiet. They could sense that this whole situation should have been more thought out before they decided to partake. Mitchelle had done several jobs for the company and never had the deal gone to this extent. Brunnel was a newbie and had done two jobs before, and both of them were with Kent whom did only four or five himself. They had tracked this kid and his family for the better part of two years steady. The case was older than that and they knew about Tristan then as well but for some reason the company just sat on it. This struck Mitchelle as odd from the get go, but with the kind of money that was laid on the table at the particular time, questions were nothing short of stupid. The other two felt the same at the time and now all three looked at each other with nothing but confusion, fear and regret. Brunnel leaned forward in his seat and put his chin next to Mitchelle's shoulder. "Should we kill the kid or just leave him somewhere after we get our money?" Kent shot a look over at him that told him what the answer should be and Mitchelle confirmed. "We aren't going to touch that kid, they will hunt us down like dogs if that boy dies. They have invested this kid for years and I'll bet they spent money we could only dream of." Kent leaned in his seat. Mitchelle took one look over and realized that he was acting like there was something missing in the conversation. "What's going on Kent?" The van was pulled over and he sat there staring at Kent waiting. "What is the story with this kid? Why have they gone to this length to get this kid, and why are we shitting our pants while you seem quiet calm for the most part Mitchelle?" Brunnel sat back realizing this was turning down the wrong road quick, he put his hand on his waist next to his pistol. Mitchelle looked out to the front of the car. Seconds seemed like minutes to Brunnel as he watched them sitting up there silent. Mitchelle turned in his seat to face Brunnel better. "They showed me these papers way back when we were introduced to each other, do you remember that day?" Kent shook his head confirming. "When you guys were lead into the office for the briefing, I was introduced to my lead officer. He gave me this folder on the kid and I thumbed through it. He said I was main contact in this operation." Brunnel took his hand away from his hip and sat up closer to the conversation. Mitchelle continued, "The paperwork read pretty clear. He was born with normal blood panels, weight and length. No problems at all until he was a little over one year old. He began to have these weird seizure spells that they had chalked up to epilepsy at first." Kent tried to care about these facts but he began to nod his head faster. "There are a few blacked out paragraphs, as usual, but later it describes his condition as "unexplainable". They get worse and he was admitted into the hospital numerous times for like episodes. Our employers step in at this time and a blood test and some other tests unreported to the Burns family were taken back to their labs. We come in and boom….."Brunnel sat back and looked out his window. He was just as confused now as he was fifteen minutes ago. Kent relaxed and Mitchelle took a deep breath. "Now", he said. "There was some word around a few employees that I happen to compensate, that the kid was wanted by the company because he could communicate with the dead." Kent didn't react at all, just stared with disbelief at Mitchelle. Brunnel on the other hand shot up and popped his head to the front a little. "Talk to the dead, what the hell are you talking about?" He could feel the tension in the vehicle rising and wondered if the mistake was too late to correct. "Apparently they have some video and scan that show some type of, of..." he paused and rubbed his chin. "Some apparition or something, but this was hearsay guys. None of which should be taken seriously." "Were did this info come from and why did they want this kid so bad that murder was an option Mitchelle?" He looked at Kent and shook his head, "I just don't know man, but I'm telling you right now, I don't think that we need to worry about dead people, really. He probably has some weird disease or condition that they want to bottle, Military or something." Kent just sat back and took all of this in. It wasn't farfetched to think that the company wouldn't go to such lengths to get a military grant or payout. They just never mentioned killing anyone before. Mitchelle even knew that this all seemed shady and killing was never an action the company spit out randomly. The lead officer seemed pretty relaxed, letting Mitchelle know who needed to be terminated. Without another word the van pulled onto the road and continued to the house. As far as Mitchelle was concerned they could die, he just wanted out. The corridor that led down to the main office was dimly lit. A bright light beamed from under the door and gave life to the last five feet of the hallway. It was dead quite in Jim Thompsons office and he worked best when all of the doctors, scientists and lawyers left for the day. His name tag hung from his shirt and covered a small coffee stain that he had made earlier in the day. He shuffled around the room anxious and thinking of just what it was he was going to tell the board at the meeting in the morning. Covering an incident that Mitchelle and the boys were about to conduct might cause questions that he couldn't answer. He didn't feel comfortable the way Mitchelle paused on the phone when he told him to rid of Stathom. It meant incompliance with the long term goal and that meant problems in its implementation. This was the first time that he had made the decision of getting rid of someone but the company let him know that he wouldn't have to worry about outcomes if his wasn't satisfactory. The boy was important to the future of the Department of Medical Development and its trustees. Every minute that passed as he wandered the room made him more nervous and he was tempted to call his advisor about the situation. He walked to his leather chair and sat down slowly, listening to the leather creek underneath him. His big oak table gave him the illusion of importance and tonight he realized how much pretending he did on a daily basis. Jim looked at the phone, envisioning talking to the advisor about the decision he had made about John. At the time he felt that the advisor would have been impressed with his actions to take charge. Only some time later to realize that he trusted this motion on a man whom chocked on the phone at the sound of it. If he didn't come through now, he would be left explaining Mitchelle's folly, or better yet, his. He glanced at papers and photographs that covered his calendar pad. A picture of Tristan smiling in his back yard, another from a x-ray room, as well as a few pictured with him and his mom out and about for the day. He couldn't understand how this entire gift was given to such a small child. You would think that a miraculous gift like that would be given to a priest or some man or women of importance. What could a boy do with the ability to talk to the dead? *Why?* Picking up some loose notes, he shuffled through some of the info he had obtained over the last few years. He was amazed at the mistakes some of the hospitals let slip by when the tests came back. His brain scans and seizure responses were off the charts. The only thing puzzlin

Jim and even some of his colleagues, were the coins. *What was with the coins?* Tristan insisted, even in the hospitals that he have the coins. During some bizarre episodes he had even shouted "Give me the coins so they can listen!" Doctors just shrugged it off as part of the reaction to the seizures and the Department's doctors couldn't make sense of it at all. They all knew it had something to do with this "Them" or "They" as Tristan referred to it. There was one incident that Jim would ponder over time and time again, a video that his lab had taken during a hospital stay last year around May. He got up from his desk and walked over to his file cabinet and scanned the top drawer for the audio/video files. He started thumbing through the alphabet reciting it like a kindergartener. He couldn't remember what hospital it was and began to wish he had sorted these out by patient name like a smart man instead of by place of incident, *Stupid bastard.* It took several minutes before he had found the right DVD and he returned to his desk and reached to boot up his computer. The flat screen on the right corner of his desk sparked to life and he closed his eyes for a second waiting to hear that famous chime of windows. He popped the DVD into the disc drive and retrieved his wireless mouse from within the mess. Sitting back in his seat he used the arm rest as his mouse pad and adjusted the volume. The video showed Tristan sitting in a white room with his mother and playing with some type of action figures. She was thumbing thru some magazine and every so often would look up at him and smile. A doctor entered the room and put down a clipboard. He asked the common questions and proceeded to look at Tristan, get vitals, etc, etc. Several minutes had passed and the doctor left them alone again. Jim couldn't remember where in the video the incident happens and he was forced to sit and watch. A nurse came in and handed his mother some papers and took Tristan out of the room. Jim watched his mother read a magazine and thought about what it was like for her to wonder what they knew was wrong with her son. If she was ever told what he could do? What would she do? She sat there oblivious to what her son was going through and what they wanted with him and that someone even wanted him. It was just a mother worrying about seizures her boy was having. The nurse returned Tristan with a lollipop and a handful of stickers. He jumped up on the bed and showed his mom what he picked out. She acted excited and he shuffled through his stack and then gave one to her which she quickly peeled and stuck to her shirt. He put them down on the bed and resumed his play as before and his mom looked at him for a few seconds and returned to his magazine. Jim sat up in his chair realizing that this was when it happened, he remembered. The camera fuzzed up a bit and the room's lights flickered. His mother looked up at the ceiling and then realized Tristan was rocking back and forth, "Tristan, honey?" The boy didn't respond and Jim turned up the volume and leaned in closer. Tristan looked up and turned his head to the right in an odd angle. His mother stood up and stared as he stood up and began to jerk his hands into his pockets feverishly. "Can you hear them mommy? They want you to listen." She circled to his side and tried to look into his eyes. Tristan pulled a quarter from his pocket and held it straight out. He smiled at her in a crooked way that made him look like an evil cartoon character. Jim was astonished at how calm she remained and wondered how many times she had been through this? He knew she was terrified, she must be. This was her son. Tristan reached his hand further to her. "You can hear them can't you? They hear you Jody, and they want to be free." Jody went back the other way and opened the door to the room. She walked out from the cameras view and Jim could hear her yell for help. Tristan just stood there facing the same way and didn't seem to respond that his mother ever left. "Oh, you can hear them and they can hear you, Jody. They have been here longer than any of you and they are waiting in the fields." Jim pause the video and looked away. "What the hell are the fields?" This was the question that everyone that has seen this video has. They were so concerned about the contortion or the coins but what about the fields? He knew that Tristan was referring to a place that actually existed in his head or he wouldn't have mentioned it, and "They" lived there. The video resumed and he watched to see if there was something he didn't see the first hundred or more times he had watched it. Tristan squeezed the coin in his hand and two nurses and the doctor from earlier raced into the room. The nurses went to grab Tristan on the arms and he let out this horrible screech that made everyone except Jody cover their ears. He looked at his mother and then dropped the coin to the floor. As soon as it hit the floor Tristan collapsed on to the bed and bounced off, hitting the floor, splitting his head open. Jody panicked, and the nurses quickly uncovered their ears and lifted the boy to the bed. Jim stopped the video and threw the mouse on his desk. He sat up and began to spread the contents of the desk out and thumb through the photos and papers. He wasn't looking for anything in particular but maybe something would jump out at him that he just didn't get before. About twenty minutes went by, and he sat back defeated once again. He looked at his wrist watch and realized it was at least four hours since he had last had contact with Mitchelle. He picked up the receiver and dialed Mitchelle's cell. A slight pause and he heard the phone pick up. Jim went into his commander mode, "So what is the progress so far Mitchelle?" When his phone rang he knew it was the lead officer and he looked at Kent with a discouraged look. He picked up his phone and flipped it open. "Mitchelle", he chimed. "Well we are on our way to the house still sir, we had to stop and discuss how we were going to get the child?" Brunnel sat in the back seat and looked out the window trying to be patient. "Right sir, we just want to get him away from Mr. Stathom first and then take care of the necessities after the boy is secure, sir." Kent shook his head and stared at Mitchelle trying to hear the other side of the conversation. "Were would you like us to meet when the child is secure?" Mitchelle nodded his head and looked over at Kent. "Yes sir, yes sir." He hung up the phone and tossed it on the dashboard. "As soon as we have the child and John is terminated we are to call him and they will send some people to retrieve the child." Brunnel looked at the back of Mitchelle's head, "Nope, it isn't going to happen Mitchelle. We won't make it out of the van, man. As soon as I get within five feet of that kid I'm going to kill John and snatch that kid and head straight for Mexico." Kent didn't have a reaction to the comment and Mitchelle could tell that he agreed. "Alright", Mitchelle said, "Sounds like that is our only plan and what then, ransom?" Kent nodded and looked back at Brunnel. Mitchelle looked at Kent and slammed on the breaks. He felt Brunnel hit the back of his seat and without hesitation Mitchelle pulled his pistol and shot Kent in the face. Brunnel fumbled for his waist holster and two shot rang from the van as it hummed silent on the vacant road. Mitchelle sat back and adjusted his seat. "We are not going to Mexico Kent!" He took a deep breath and looked back at Brunnel who was slumped over and bleeding from his head. "I'm going to get paid my friends and I don't care what happens to that bastard kid." He put the van in drive and drove into the night. He retrieved his cell phone from the dash and called his lead Officer. When he told him of what they had planned to do Jim, thanked him for looking out for the company's interest and that he would be well compensated for his loyalty. As far as Mitchelle was concerned, the boy could die. He just wanted his money.

CHAPTER 8

As dark as it was, the field gave off a soft glow. On the horizon the stars and dark blue skyline made it seem like a peaceful watercolor hanging in a museum, being of no harm, just pleasure. The fact was that within the grass the silhouettes awaited the call of the master, the one that promised them salvation from the wait in the fields. The one whom controlled the old man's hanging tree and the house that he dwelled in so long ago. People have come and gone over the years and they have all suffered at the hands of the master. No one has ever taken them out from the field, set them free as the master promised. The night felt different and the master has shown them that the boy was the key. Elysium would let them go and they could once again be with those whom have passed before them. The boy knew the way, they were sure of it. The master was sure of it. The only fear was the house. With the farmer's soul so long gone from their deadened eyes, they were sure the house would ultimately be of no issue. The tree was the sole incarnation of the master and has its roots yearning to be at rest, to die. The master wouldn't hear of it and it was the only thing that kept the family in order.Everyone that lived in that wretched house was in fear of that tree and the master kept it so. Jody was not the first to want it torn from the foundation. Many have died at the hands of the master trying and all have failed. They had warned the master of the impatience that has grown amongst them. Years of waiting while more souls gathering in the field, souls from the house and souls from the master. They had never questioned where the master had come from and they knew that he was not one of them. He was here before. Even the souls that wandered the fields when they first stepped in its soil never knew where the master came from. Whispers have said that it was the field itself in a form they could understand and not in the interest of setting them free. But others have passed and the field must have mercy. They stood on the horizon, far from the house and watched the master at the edge of the yard. He had a plan and they would rejoice at the sight of the boy. He would set them free as the master told them. They would pass the Elysium fields and into the arms of their loved ones and children that have passed. Families of the families would unite and embrace one another in a place that no man could witness with living eyes. So they watched the master stand at the edge of the yard. He was the key and they entrusted in him the damning of their souls. The ferry man must be paid and they had no gold. But the master spoke of this boy with the coins, the power. They have seen the coins and they whispered to him to make the others listen, to let him come to them and show them the way. He would be safe with his family, and they could leave the damned fields and the murky soil that lay upon their feet. This was the promise of the master. The boy had come into the fields and with fury he had left, killing his father and retreating back to the house. When the master was called upon to stop this he was hidden from sight. When he returned he had taken the boy's father and removed his skin for himself. This is what he said must be done for the boy to trust him. With trust he will pay the way to salvation and the ferry man will be pleased to let them pass. There was more whisper of the master. It was said that he killed the boy's father and that he let the boy go. We are blinded from such things and can only see what the master lets us see but what we hear in the grass speaks the truth, if we listen. We warned the master and he took listen to our concern and prompted us to have the faith in him to bring the boy to us. He was angered at our questions and threatened to leave us and the fields to rot and so the word is all that is left with the master. The horizon played tricks on the eyes of the living as if they could see an end to the world they lived in. This was the illusion of the fields. The fields inhabit the entire world and beyond it, the salvation of the damned. No one has returned from salvation to tell of its beauty and no one has left the living and passed the fields, untouched by its soil. The book of man that tells of its stay in wormy earth has little effect on the souls that inhabit the fields. The fields are forever, and the fields sprout no fruit without payment. The ferry man is blind and only feels the metal of coin and the tears of the wicked. He holds all that there is to the other side, and cannot speak in visuals. Many have come and claimed to know the way but have been stranded here by their own ignorance and selfishness. All pay the price for the selfish in the fields and until the master came, they say too many years hardened the soil beneath the feet. No one shall pass. But what will be done if the master is a false one? There were whispers of burying him in the fields where he could never be found by a living or non living soul again,where his cries to be free can never touch even the soil or the grasses that carry him away from the soil. He ignored our warnings and shown teeth, threatening anyone whom stands before the master with question. But we listen sometimes. Even the grasses tell us the truths that others hide under the skin. The grasses whisper. And sometimes we listen.

CHAPTER 9

It was different. They way the air smelled and the sounds that called to her. It was like a dream, but she knew that she was far from that. The tree had grabbed her and she could feel her eyes exploding, her brain screaming for air. Now, with what seemed a second from death, she was here, in the fields. The grass caressed her feet and the soil seemed soft and warm. The sky was a very dark blue and she circled, looking around, she could see the house, far away. The tree stood at the edge of the yard and played in the wind. The stranger stood at the edge of the yard staring into the fields as if he was waiting for something. Jody turned to the horizon and stared at it in confusion. It didn't seem the same. She began to walk towards the house as the grass parted before her feet. The soil sank between her toes, and she realized she had only one shoe on. Without stopping she kicked the other shoe away and began to run for the house. Her chest was beginning to heave and burn as she picked up the pace. *What the hell is going on?* When her lungs gave out she bent down to catch her breath and went to one knee. Peering up at the house she realized she had gotten no closer than when she started the sprint. She began to lie down and tears filled her eyes. Jody's body shook and her hands punched the ground. "Where is my son!" she began to scream into the soil. It wasn't listening. The grass folded around her and she curled up into a ball weeping. *Why are you doing this, what are you?* She waited for the pain and it never came. Wherever she was, they didn't hear her. "This is not true." Jody looked up and then sat up really quick looking around. "We are here Jody, and you are with us." She stood up and circled. All around her there were figures, black as the sky, silhouettes with no faces that she could make out. "Who are you?" she whipped. "We are the inhabitants of the field as are you now." She stepped around and her mind began to reel. "What do you mean, me?" "Yes, you are part of the fields now and must come with us to wait for the master." Jody began to panic. "Do not worry, your other is here with us as well, he waits for you to acknowledge. We know of your Tristan and he will help us all reach the other side of Elysium." "Other?" Jody thought to herself. From behind one of the dark forms a voice called out. "Jody." She stood momentarily and then dropped to her knees holding her mouth, "Dustin?" She looked around her in the direction of the voice and couldn't see him beyond the black figures. "Where are you?" Tears made it hard for her to see in front of her,so she smudged them away with her wrist. "We are dead honey. We are part of the fields now. Tristan is there on the other side and we have to call to him." Her face turned stone suddenly and she stood up whipping the remainder of her tears away on her sleeve. "How dare you use me to get to my son, I will not call to him, you liars!" The figures spread apart and some of them disappeared entirely. A figure began to emerge from the crowd and Jody froze, eyes wide. Dustin walked up to her and smiled looking straight into her eyes. "We are here Jody, you and I. Don't fight it. I watched the tree take your life and the pain blackened my heart. You're here now and we need to call to our son. His is alone." She touched his face slowly and looked into his eyes. A slight mist wrapped around his body, much like the strangers. He put his hand over hers and looked towards the house. "He is there for us Jody." Looking back at her, a mist began to fill her face and she calmed before him. "We will help our Tristan. He will not follow us into the field, Dustin. He will live and have babies of his own and cherish life." Dustin smiled down at her and looked back at the others. "My son will help you but you must not take him with us. The master doesn't need my boy, nor do you, you just need him to tell the ferry man, that's all." The figures stood still. Dustin knew they had to take the boy and it wasn't his decision. One stepped forward and the darkness faded around him. He was a young black man, strong in build and his face was somber. "I used to live there when the farmer was our master." Jody looked at Dustin, confused. "We were hung from that tree there," he pointed towards the house. "All of us here have lived in that house and all of us have died there. The master says we must have the boy for the ferry man to take us to our families. He speaks the truth, sir." Dustin walked to him and placed his hand on his shoulder. "I understand. The master has led you to believe it is the only way that you may find salvation. But my son can pay the ferry man and still live his life can't he?" The young man looked at him and bowed his head. "No one living has ever seen the ferry man and walked back to the living sir, no one." Another figure stepped forward and walked up to Dustin. He was a slightly older man and dressed like he was from the sixties and was stern in his looks. "He is right." The young boy walked away into the darkness. Dustin watched him and then looked back to the older man. "Your son will not live if he sees the ferry man. He will be taken to salvation with all of us, and you." Jody looked at the man and shook her head, "He is just a boy." The man turned and walked away leaving them standing there in the field. The silhouettes, one by one, began to fade into the darkness and whispered into the night, "Listen, he will guide us." Jody stepped away from Dustin and faced the house. The master stood on the yards edge never moving a muscle as if frozen in time. "What do you suppose that man really is?" Dustin look at her, "He is no man Jody. He is the taker of souls. I don't think he was ever a man. The people of the fields fear him and speak of him as if he were since time began. I believe he may have been." The tree danced with grass and the master suddenly turned towards the house. "NO!" Jody began to run towards the house again at full speed. Her lungs did not burn and her legs felt light. The house just stayed in the distance but she just kept pushing herself to get to her son. "Jody", Dustin said standing right next to her. She stopped and stared towards the house, never looking at Dustin, and wept. Dustin felt her shoulder and bowed his head. In the distance, a figure emerged from the grass. Slumped over slightly, it looked different than the other dark figures. Jody ignored it as Dustin tried to make out what it was. When it came within ten feet of them, Dustin tapped Jody and she looked to see black saucer-like eyes staring at her. It was short, lanky, and quick on its feet. "I know of your boy sir." Its language was harsh. It turned its head to the side and let out a clicking sound like chatter. Some figures behind it sat on the edge of the darkness. "The master will not let you take the boy with you. He has other plans for him you understand?" Jody got closer to Dustin. "Who are you?" The creature clicked and snapped as it flung its hand behind, waving off the lurkers in the distance. "We are the keepers of the souls, sir. The master does not control us or the field, we let him see. I was in your house from the beginning." "When," Dustin asked. "From the time the fields were laid, sir. Long before that wretched tree or house stood over this land. We were here when the foundation was set." "Why does he want our son?" The creature stepped closer to Dustin, tilting its head at Jody. "You are pretty like your boy has said, very nice." Dustin pressed Jody tighter to him and the creature could smell the fear. "Do not concern yourself with us, you are part of the field now and we don't have a need to harm you. I have a solution." They stood staring at the creature without response. "It is simple." It continued. "The boy needs to get the master to us and we will pass you along to salvation and leave the boy behind. We have no need for him or his coins." Jody looked past him and into the distance at the shadows, "But why?" It looked at her and bared its teeth and grimaced at her. "I have watched your boy since you brought him home. I held him at night while you slept in your bed. That is why he likes the night walks so much. I even brought him here to the fields and he listens and sees us. You could not and did not listen when we spoke to you. You did not listen when we spoke through him. He is the key and we can return home if the fields are empty." "Where is home?" Dustin said. The creature looked back, and the others slowly showed themselves in the field's dim light. They were just as the other and walked slightly hunched. The creature looked at Dustin and stepped closer with its eyes widened and teeth bearing, it growled at him and spoke softly. "Hell sir." The master paced on the edge of the field and looked out at Dustin and Jody standing alone. *Where was the boy?* As Jody turned, the master appeared behind Dustin and looked around as the fog lifted from his body. His grin was absent now and the grass almost laid flat at the presence of him. Jody began to back up a few steps and Dustin spun facing him, no more than two feet away. "How do you like the playground Dustin, You and the wife having a good time?" Dustin backed up and looked around the fields. The others were gone as if they knew he was coming. "Where is Tristan?" he smiled slightly. Jody walked up next to Dustin, "We don't knowyou are looking for him too." The master breathed in deep and held it for a few seconds. When he let it out he stared at them annoyed. "You see, the boy is the way for these lost souls here and it appears to me that neither of you see the importance within that." "We understand that he cannot come with us and that you will make him." Jody answered. "He is just a little boy!" Dustin pleaded. "I am sure there is a way that we can get us all to the other side, you must know that." The master paced back and forth looking at the ground as if he were in deep thought. "Well", he stopped and looked up. "The only way was for you to listen and quite frankly that was a worthless plight now, wasn't it. You are now both here and the boy there," he pointed and looked towards the house. "Listening is not an option, and for that, he will have to die." Jody grabbed Dustin's arm and stepped forward. "We know what it is you want, they have told us." "They?" the master smirked. "As in the inhabitants of the field, they know fare well what I can do and promised for them. They tell tales here to pass the time and one of those tales is me." He leaned closer. "But I assure you what you hear is just that, a tale. I am the master here and I own these fields." "But why did you need us to listen, you just wanted our son." The master looked hard at Dustin and walked in three quick steps eye to eye with him. Dustin tilted his head back a little startled, for one, at the fact that he was that close to this thing and two, that he didn't do harm. His breath smelled of something unnatural and hot, death on the highway. His eyes glanced back and forth, dark and hollow into Dustin's. "Listening would have prevented the others from questioning what needed to be done." Dustin looked away and the master backed his face up, straitening his posture. Jody looked at Dustin and then back at the master, "what do you mean, what needed to be done?" He shot a glare at her as if she had appeared out of nowhere and pushed Dustin to the side and pointed at her. Dustin caught his balance and went to his side. Without hesitation the master grabbed him by the arm and tossed him six feet away to the ground like he was a mere distraction. "What needs to be done in the fields is none of your concern dear lady," he grabbed the back of her hair and yanked her to one side. She balanced on one foot and winced as he tugged. Dustin rolled to his side and got to his feet. He didn't know if he should attack or just stand and wait. "The fields", he continued, "is a place of death, waiting and suffering. All those who inhabit it are waiting for their salvation and their ticket out. Like your world, ours is full of deceit and spite." He turned to Dustin. "Do you think John has good intention for your boy?" Dustin's mind began to race. "Yes," he smiled, "the same John that you entrusted. Mr. Stathom is his name I, believe. Again, do you think he has good intentions?" Dustin was confused and tried to make sense of why John had anything to do with his boy. "Stop thinking so hard and let me fill in the gap," He let go of Jody's hair and she righted herself and backed away. "John has your boy as we speak but his intentions are with another. A group of individuals who would love nothing more to pry his little skull wide open and get to what's inside, they know all about you and your family, and John is being paid quite nicely to make sure Tristan ends up in the right hands." Dustin stepped forward, "How do you know this is true?" The master looked out the corner of his eyes. "We know all about your world, we used to live there, remember?" He smiled and looked back at the house. The night sky engulfed the horizon and made it look old and dead. "Don't worry Dustin, he won't even have the chance to engage in such activity. The boy will be mine." He turned and began to walk back towards the house. "Oh," he paused. "The same goes for your friends from the hospital Jody. They don't have a chance." He walked into shadows, they watched as he disappeared before their eyes. "Jody ran over to Dustin and looked around the field. "Are you ok?" He shook his head and looked toward the house. Tristan was alone out there somewhere and they needed to find their way beyond this field, back to Tristan. "You have no way to save him," a voice came from behind them. When they turned around a sea of silhouettes scattered the field. "Don't worry Mr. Burns, your boy is strong and the master doesn't realize just how." Dustin walked closer to them and they seemed to float back a step for every step he advanced. He stopped, turned and just walked away towards the house. Jody stared at them for a second and then caught up with Dustin never looking back. "We have no way to him Jody," he stopped and looked to the house. She knew that as much as she wanted to believe that they could do something for Tristan, they were here and there was nothing they could do to get there. Mitchelle drove on and thought about what he was going to do when he arrived at the house. He was disturbed at how the events had turned out so far. He was sure that he could get the kid without incident from John but if needed, he looked over at Kent and returned his glance to the road. The night seemed like it went on forever, and the drive followed suit. He would have to dump the bodies and the van. *Maybe the company will do that for me?* He could say that with confidence a few days back but now, he wasn't so sure. The lead officer was expecting a call when the boy was in his possession and Mitchelleknew they would do anything to make that happen. His life was no more valuable than the two other dead men in his van. He began to think that maybe the idea of Mexico might not have been a bad idea. That was all behind him and now he would have to get out of this alone. He passed a road sign that said, "Welcome toClumbens-Ville" and he sat up in his seat and rolled down the window, letting the air shock him back into reality. He would need to call them soon and let them know he was there. He reached for his phone and paused for a second watching the road. He shook his head and cleared the idea of Mexico as he grabbed the phone and flipped it open.

CHAPTER 10

The house sat quite as the smoke bellowed from its innards. The night ignored the happenings and called to the nightly inhabitants. Animals scrambled in the bush on their routine hunts and the flying monsters roamed the air on the same mission. The tree reached into the night and scrapped at the skyline as it swayed with the field. The history that stood upon these ground all came together and it was time that the history came to its end. The master stood in the back yard and took all of this in. "My old friend," he looked at the tree. It bent in his direction paying homage to its owner. He had taken care of that tree since he heard the screams of the men, children, and women hanging from its soulless branches and now it breaths with him. The inhabitants of the field shall never know how many souls he had sacrificed to give that tree its life. The house on the other hand was nothing but a shell used to store the living, so it may weed out the useless until it found the one. When they had bought the house the fields had remained quiet for quite some time. When the others began to speak of this child that could hear them he knew that it would need to be silenced. As the owner of the fields, no one shall leave him to wander its edges alone. Centuries had passed and the ferry man had not passed one soul. If one had gotten through, the others would begin to speak of salvation again. The house stood there and mocked the master. It didn't need to bend like the tree and keep the secrets from the field, from the master. He looked back at the field and smiled at Dustin and Jody, as they stood alone, waiting to see the fate of their young boy. The master knew that it would easy to pry him from John, and smite him right in front of the field's edge, so the inhabitants know they were at his mercy. They would stay with him for eternity and secrets would be hushed forever more. The river will run dry and the ferry man will ground his boat, leaving the others with him. No one shall pass into salvation. He needed to find where the house was hiding the boy. He must be within its walls and he would tear them down one board at a time to get to him. He walked across the yard and stopped at the porch's stairs. "You can hide him all you like. In the end he will succumb to me, and I will burn you to the ground." The house stood quiet and the master climbed the stairs to the back door and stomped three timed on its wood planks. "Tristan!" he yelled at the top of his lungs. The animals scurried from the bushes and the air was filled with a screech that made Jody and Dustin fall to their knees, and the inhabitants of the field come from the shadows. They knew that this was a sound none of them have heard. This was the end. The sound broke off and echoed into the horizon shaking the sky. "Your not to worry Mr. Burns, your boy will return us to our salvation and the master won't have any way to stop it. The ferry man waits for us all Mr. Burns, all of us." The master walked up to the door and kicked it in with such furry it toppled over the kitchen table and splintered against the wall and into the hallway. The smoke escaped and revealed a dark and desolate room that once held refuge for this wretched family. He had winced in disgust at the thought of it, and walked in scouring the room. Nothing but dust, door fragments and broken dishes covered the room.He threw things around the room as he hunted for any sign of life. "Tristan!" he yelled again. The house shook and the fields echoed. Jody began to welcome the sound for as long as they heard that sound their boy was safe. John looked down the driveway and tried hard to spot his car, *shit*. Tristan stood on the side of the drive and stared at the house listening to the stranger smashing things and screaming his name. John needed to get the hell out of here and somehow he needed to talk Tristan into coming with him. Telling him that his parents were ok was the last trick he wanted to try. The kid was too smart for that and there would be no way to convince him after a lie like that. "They will come for me sir, I know it." "What makes you think they will," John questioned. Tristan turned and walked into the dark away from the house, towards the road. He stopped when he thought the stranger would not see them from the house and he went the side of the drive. "I have not heard them in awhile and think they are waiting for the stranger to go. He is not like them, and I think he wants to hurt them." John was shocked at how calm he was, but yet when he spoke his voice trembled. He didn't think the boy was in shock and he would rather have that be the case. Anything else meant "them", whoever "they" were. "We should probably go back to my car and see if we can call for help." Tristan didn't respond in any way and John stood quietly waiting for something. "Tristan," he realized the boy was in a daze looking at the ground. John rubbed his pant legs and looked around. "Do not touch the boy Mr. Stathom." John bent in and tried to get a look at Tristan's face. Tristan stared at the ground with his eyes glazed. "The masterhas talked to his parents about your plans Mr. Stathom." He backed up from the boy and looked around to see who was controlling this. "What do you know about what my plans are Tristan?" "We know about the others, the people who want the boy for his secrets." John walked away from the boy and looked towards the house. "Who are you and what do you know?" Tristan looked up at John and smiled a crooked smile, "We know what type of person you are Mr. Stathom, and the master has plans for you, much like the plans you had for the boy." He pointed at Tristan and shook his finger. "You know nothing of what I plan to do and when I find Jody and Dustin..." Tristan cut him off and looked back at the house. "...You know nothing of this boy's mother and father." He paused and turned his head and widened his eyes. "We have spoken with them and they concern for their son." John began to panic and he looked towards the house. "Who is that in there?" Tristan never took his gaze from him and showed his teeth in an odd manner that made John sweat, "The master Mr. Stathom." He backed away more, turned and walked towards the road. Sweat poured from his forehead, he looked back as Tristan stared at him smiling. He stopped when he felt safe, *what the hell?* Looking at the ground he fumbled for his cigarettes again and began to mutter to himself when he heard a thud. He looked up and saw Tristan lying in the driveway. He stared and didn't know what to do. Was that it? Was the episode over? He slowly took a few steps and noticed he was stirring a little, "Tristan?" The boy turned on his side and coughed. John ran up and bent to his side, "You ok?" He looked around and wiped his brow. Tristan moaned and looked up at him, "What are your plans, sir?" He looked at Tristan and ran his fingers across his mouth,"To get you to your mother and father." Tristan leaned away and began to get to his knees. "Where are my parents? Can we go now?" He helped Tristan up, "Yeah, we need to find them Tristan. We need to find them now."He began to walk towards the house and Tristan followed. Are they in the house sir? What about the master?" John stopped again and looked at Tristan. "I don't know Tristan, I hope we find them before he finds you. What do you know about the master?" Tristan shrugged his shoulders and looked at the house. "Maybe we should go to fields, I know the fields. We could be safe there." "Is that were 'they' are?" Tristan shook his head then grabbed John's hand. He looked down at Tristan and realized that he needed to get this kid to Mitchelle before things got out of control. Whatever or whoever it was that was in that house would kill him for this boy and he wasn't here for confrontation. Tristan pulled him toward the house and John followed, thinking of a way to get him away. If he grabbed, him he was sure to scream and someone would hear, Jody, Dustin, the master. "We will go around the house once and if we do not see your mom and dad we head for my car, deal?" Tristan didn't answer, but gripped John's hand harder as he headed for the side of the house. John felt comfort that he wasn't headed for the front door but knew Tristan would not abandon the house easy. The dirt snapped and crunched beneath their feet and John tried to walk as quiet as he could. It seemed that every time the noise from within the house would pause, their steps would be at their loudest. Tristan just tugged him along and didn't concern himself with keeping the approach silent. It was apparent that although Tristan was afraid of the thing inside, he wasn't about to let that interfere with finding his parents. "Listen," John stopped him. "I don't think this is such a good idea, Tristan. We need to get back to the car and call for help." He ignored John and let his hand go, advancing forward. They were only two to three yards from the house, and that was as close as John was willing to get. "Tristan," He whispered loudly. When Tristan reached the side of the house he turned only once to look at John before he went the side and disappeared into the shadows. John scuffled across the drive and entered the shadows after him. The side of the house was bellowing smoke and it made John squint. Tristan wasn't there and John thought that seemed odd that he could get around to the back without that thing in the house noticing. *Where are you boy?* "Tristan," he called out,nothing. Swooshing the smoke from in front of his face he made his way to the backside of the house. It was damp in the shadows and he could see the tree at the edge of the yard bending into the wind as if it were dancing. There at the edge of the field in the middle of the yard stood Tristan. He just stood there looking out into the field. He went to advance and a door creaked from his left. He turned and saw a man step out onto the porch. John backed into the shadows a bit and began to look around for anything, a stick, something to protect himself if he were to be discovered. *If this asshole thinks he's going to take this kid from me?*John watched as he stood on the porch and watched Tristan. Without word he floated into the air and landed as if he were in slow motion onto the grass. "Tristan," his voice was dark and airy. John realized that whatever this thing was, it wasn't human. His heart began to pound the side of his chest and his forehead dripped sweat into his eyes. Tristan turned slowly and faced the man. "Your parents are looking for you, I know where they are." The man stood perfectly still as if not to scare the boy off. John wiped the sweat with his sleeve and rubbed his hands on his pants. "Would you like me to take you to them?" Tristan looked out into the field, then back to the stranger. "They are there, in the fields." The master smiled at him and put his hand on his chin. "What makes you think that?" He paused for a brief second. "I am truly sorry about our encounter earlier, it's them. They are my flock and I need to save them. It was desperation." Tristan looked back out to the field and then at his feet. "Show me my mom and dad." The master ran his hand over his face and when Tristan looked up he saw his mother staring back at him. "Honey, it's ok." Tristan went to run to her and stopped in mid stride. "Come to me honey, I miss you." He stepped back and eyeballed the stranger. "You lie," he said softly. His mothers face contorted into a scowl and twisted into the face of his father. Tristan jumped a little and stared into his eyes. "You get over here now boy and do as your mother says." Tristan turned and ran straight into the field. The master gave chase and before he could enter the field John stepped out, "Run Tristan!" The master turned and looked at John surprised. "Well," he smiled. "Mr. Stathom, here to provide guidance to the family. Where are your counter parts?" John stepped to the side a bit to get into the light better. "I don't know who you are working for pal but you aren't taking that boy." He sounded confident and he stared at the strange man with someone with authority. The fear in his chest built up behind his eyes and he was about to collapse. The stranger looked him up and down and then gave out a loud and insulting laugh. "Is that so? Well I believe you could make that a possibility, although I don't think you have any guts to make it a reality." He took a few steps towards John and bore his teeth. John took a deep breath, as he looked into the viper's mouth, sharp, bloody teeth with a tongue whipping back and forth between them. He looked out to the field to see if Tristan had gotten far enough away, "Listen," he said. "I don't know what this is all about but we can make this work for the both of us, I'm sure." The master closed his mouth and stopped dead in his tracks. He was surprised at how calm the man was even though his death was imminent. He smiled and decided to let the salesman give it a shot. He put his hands up and tilted his head. "This sounds interesting." John relaxed slightly and smiled back, "Ok, I didn't think you were a fool." He didn't think getting cocky was the smartest thing to do but now that he had some control here he needed to keep it. "Go on," the master crouched down to the yard and folded his hands between his legs. He stared at John with his eyes squinted but his meaning was understood. John thought that this could go either way and the man wasn't going to negotiate, it was being convincing or end up buried in that field. "I understand you want the kid too," John straightened himself to look big and confident. "I need that kid as well and I'm sure there is a way for us to both get what it is we want." Now the master opened his eyes a little wider. Maybe he had underestimated the imagination and skill of this human. He unfolded his hand and let them rest on his knees, waiting. John wiped some of the sweat from his brow noticing how stained his sleeve was from doing so often tonight. "I have a group of people who would love nothing more than to get a hold of this kid, maybe we could work something out," "Like what," the master interrupted. John paused and took a breath. "Well, we…we could get the boy to them and you could wait nearby. When I have received my money then you could come out and do whatever it is you do and take the child." The master put his left hand to the grass and ran his fingers through it collecting moisture. He put it near his face, his tongue slithering from his jagged mouth, licking his fingers. "The field is my home Mr. Stathom, do you realize just who it is I am. It seems you think I'm more like you." John looked around the ground and ran his fingers through his hair,he could smell his own sweat and was damn sure whatever that thing was, he could do the same. "Well, rest assured Mr. Stathom, I will get the boy with or without your help." He stood up and looked out towards the field. The grass played in the wind and in the distance he could smell Tristan, his tongue responded by licking the air and flicking in and out of his mouth. John had made an error and knew the thing would never let him walk away from this yard. "Sir," his voice slightly trembled. "I do believe that I have been a fool and would like to part with this situation." The master started to smile that Cheshire grin and walked towards John slowly, "Part from the situation? Well, that's interesting Mr. Stathom. A few moments ago you were planning a heist with me and now?" He stopped several feet from John and shook his head. "You can go I guess. I have no need for you and I don't think you have the fighters will to get the child. Do you?" He realized that the master's sarcastic tone was making him the fool and obliged in it, "No sir, I do not." "Then I see no need for you to be here and you can make your way back to your hole." John stared at him for a few seconds as the master looked out to the field ignoring his presence now. As he walked away the hairs on his neck stood up and he began to panic as he realized how close to death he was. Tristan and his family were involved in something that he could never figure or explain within his lifetime. They would die and he would bury this story, and get as far away from Elysiumas his money would take him. He paused for only a brief second and looked to see the thing standing there, looking out upon the field. The wind blew smoke past his eyes and he brushed it away and turned making for the front yard. As he ran out into the drive he looked around as he sprinted for the road. He stopped at the end of the drive and looked back at the house, *what was that thing?* A whisper filled the air, "Not even your dreams could answer that question Mr. Stathom." He spun to see the master's mouth gaping wide and his teeth extended like daggers. John put his hands up and tried to back up as the master's tongue shot out and pierced his eye, penetrating his skull and escaping out the back of his head. His body fell to the dirt and the master licked the air and let the blood drip down his tongue into his open mouth. "It has occurred to me that it would be a shame for you to leave this fine establishment without the proper tour." He lifted John's corpse by the tuft of hair on the back of his head and drug him down the drive, walking upright and with no sign of struggling, he whistled into the night air and was overjoyed that there would be one more for the field tonight.

CHAPTER 11

Mitchelle could see the house from the long road and stopped about a mile away. There was smoke coming from all sides of it and he was looking around to see if police or fire trucks flashed in the distance. He couldn't say he was shocked that there wasn't, this was as far out into the boonies as one could get in these parts and you'd be lucky if anyone came or cared to. He retrieved his phone and called the lead officer. The buzz from his phone assured him just how far this place out was and even when a voice shot over the earpiece, he wasn't sure of its stability. "I'm about a mile out sir. The house seems to be on fire," a voice overtook his conversation. "What do you mean the house is on fire?" "Well, there is smoke coming from everywhere but there isn't a sign of any police or," "Listen to me," the voice interrupted again, "do you know if anyone is even at the house at this point?" "As I said sir, I'm about a mile out and I wanted to call to find out what it is I should do." The line grew silent, all but the crackling, and Mitchelle waited knowing to give him a minute to respond. He already sounded very unhappy and this could fall back on him at any moment. "Sir?" he couldn't wait any longer. "You need to get down there and find the boy Mitchelle, kill the parents I don't give a shit, just get the kid." The phone hung up and he was left sitting in the dark, shocked at the response. He could hear the fear in the man's voice, which told him that there were more people involved in this thanjust him and the company. His mind raced at all the possibilities that could turn out here tonight and none of them seemed fair at the moment. *Who else was involved?* He pulled over to the side of the road to sit for a second and gather his senses. Looking over at Kent he realized that the company would do nothing for him regarding the two bodies, and he would have to rid of them himself. He turned off the van and got out of the car. He could smell the burning wood from the house and gave a quick glance. Taking off his jacket and hanging it from the antenna, he opened the passenger door and let Kent's body slide to the ground making a thud as his head smacked the shoulder's concrete. "Let's see what we got here bud," he flipped him over and began to search through his pants pockets. He extruded some gum, a piece of folded paper with a number on it and a couple of pennies. He looked at the number, tossing the others to the ground. It wasn't a number he was familiar with and he walked around the front to get his cell. When he dialed the number he was disappointed to hear the opening hours for Chinese Express take out. Circling around to the passenger side again he tossed the paper and pocketed his phone. The pocket didn't give much either and filled his hand with a rubber band, for what, he could only guess, a candy wrapper and a lighter. His jacket pockets gave him twenty bucks and a pack of smokes as well as a cell phone, which he threw as far as he could out into the night. He dragged the body into the ditch and looked around for a good place to hide the bodies. It was so dark he couldn't make out much and he would have to just rely on dragging them far enough out that maybe a dog or something would eat most of them before they were discovered. Climbing into the van he sat down and caught his breath knowing that it was going to be a chore dragging Brunnel's body out. Hopefully there was more to gain than twenty bucks and some smokes. When he tugged the body a moaned came out that made him jump straight out of the van and pull his piece. *What the?* He peered into the van and could see Brunnel move a little. It amazed him that he survived this long in the van bleeding the way he did. His head was gaping open and Mitchelle was sure it was a lethal hit. He climbed into the van and pointed his gun. He put it down and looked out the van towards the house. If he discharged that weapon someone was going to hear it and he would have limited time to get the hell out of dodge. He put his piece away and looked at Brunnel for a second, "Ahhhh," He moaned and grabbed Brunnel around his neck. As he choked the man he could hear him gurgling but there was no fight, he wanted to die. When the last breath of air left him, Mitchelle dragged him out and searched him, finding nothing of any value. He drug the bodies about fifty feet out, returning to the van to rest for a few moments. The smell made him think of camping when he was with his father as a boy. He looked around and couldn't come up with a valid solution of how his life came to this. Like most people it was at first about money and then about a lot of money. He chuckled as he thought about it and wrested his arm on the steering wheel. Lighting one of Kent's cigarettes, he rubbed his palm on his forehead and stared at the smoking house. The kid was probably gone as well as the family and he wouldn't be able to find them at this point. He would make that call and probably end up next to Kent and Brunnel. He was starting to think that maybe the company could handle this one on their own. When the officer hung up with him he seemed more worried than he was and that told him that they were answering to someone, butwhom? Probably some government company, name to be excluded, that wasn't about to take any excuses from them about the boy's situation. They didn't seem to plan this out very well and looking out in the direction of his two former partners, he didn't either. As he took a drag from his cigarette, he contemplated just what it was he was going to do about this whole situation. He even began to imagine that it was the company who set fire to the house and now tried to lure him down to rid of him as well. He frowned and gave a disgusted look towards the house, taking long drags on his smoke. "You would like that wouldn't you? Get me down there and then bury me in the fire, oops, arson turns deadly as man is burned alive." He tossed his cigarette out to the front of the car and watched as the sparks bounced on the road. "I don't think so boys." He started the van and put it into drive and sat for a few seconds. This was it. This was the decision that would end his career in this business for good. He wasn't quite sure he wanted to do that, but in light of the circumstances, there was not time like the present. He looked out toward where he had dumped the bodies and then lit another cigarette. Retrieving his cell phone, he dialed the officer's number one last time. It felt like the longest ring tone he had ever heard in his life, when the voice came over the earpiece he paused. "Yeah, it's Mitchelle." "Have you arrived?" the man said. Mitchelle puffed on his smoke and looked toward the house. The smoke rose and turned the already black sky darker. "No," he exhaled. "As a matter of fact I don't believe they are there anymore." The lines were silent and then in a stern voice the man crackled, "Now you listen to what it is I am saying Mitchelle, get down there and find that boy or your life will be reduced as is your pay every second you waste my time." He continued to stare at the house and enjoy his cigarette. "I don't think that's going to be a problem sir," he pulled onto the road and turned the van around. As he drove away he looked at the house in the rearview and wondered just what it was he was driving away from. "Goodbye sir." he said and tossed the phone out the window. He enjoyed that cigarette and knew he would enjoy many more. *I'm driving away from nothing, that's what, nothing.* The cell phone lay in the road and into the night the officer yelled for Mitchelle. The light from the cell would die hours later than the taillights as Mitchelle headed for Mexico. He just knew Brunnel and Kent could have joined him. They would have enjoyed it, he was sure.

CHAPTER 12

Jody circled the field watching Tristan as he made his way through the grass, looking back for the stranger. Dustin ran beside him waving his arms and calling out to his boy but Tristan just kept running and every so often he would stop and bend over trying to catch his breath. The stranger was nowhere to be seen and Tristan knew that he wasn't far behind if not in front of him already. Jody held her hand out, "Tristan!" He stopped and looked in her direction and stood wide-eyed. *He hears me.* Dustin looked back at her and stood in front of his boy trying to get him to see him there. He stopped and crouched in front of his son and saw the silhouettes of a small man coming from out of the darkness. Before he got very far out Tristan turned and confronted the stalker. "Ahh, it is me Tristan from the basement, remember?" Tristan breathed slowly and relaxed a little. "Where did you go that night, I stayed up for so long hoping to see you again." The creature looked at him with his big eyes and nodded in sorrow. "I have been hiding from the master and he knows where it is you are boy. He is not tricked that easily, but you do not need to fear him." His parents didn't move a muscle and waited to see if they had noticed them there. "It is your mother and father that I have spoken to and they are here in the fields with you tonight." Tristan looked around trying to see. The creature smiled, "You cannot see them, they are part of the field now and will pass to the other side when you come to give salvation." He turned back to the creature and then to the house. "Are they dead?" The stalker confirmed his question, raised his hand, "do not weep for them. I have told them that you were strong and that you would bring them all home." "Who are you," Tristan asked. The creature paused and looked up at him and showed his teeth in a friendly manner. "We are the keepers of the field. We dwell not here but take those who deserve not the salvation." The boy looked around, "Where?" He could hear the grass bend in the air as the creature walked up face to face with him, "To hell Tristan." He stepped back as two others came into sight. Jody began to panic and Dustin stood up and began to yell Tristan's name trying to get his or their attention. "Calm, calm boy, we have no need for you for if we did I could have taken you a long time ago, yes?" The two other creatures joined the first at his side and Jody walked up and stopped Dustin as they watched. "The master wants to keep the people here Tristan." The other two clicked and clucked as the first hissed at them turning his head. "If that is so then we can no longer stay here and must return home. We don't want to go home. It is much better here, in the fields, watching the humans suffer as they do." Tristan thought of stories he heard from the bible, "You are demons?" They looked around with their saucer eyes, "We are keepers of the fields, collectors of the damned." Tristan understood why that term may seem insulting to them and gave them a concerned look. "What is it that I am supposed to do?" They smiled at him and looked toward the house. "You have the payment that the ferry man needs." Tristan looked towards the horizon, "The coins?" Laughter filled the field and the creature got even closer as if he had to whisper in his ear. "The coins were the message of payment for the mortals to hear. They never listened and for that they do not understand the payment." Tristan stood confused more than before and took a breath in thinking. "It is you boy, your soul." Dustin and Jody looked at the creatures and felt helpless to their son. He would die at the hands of the master and not even those things could save him from the fields. Tristan shook his head, "I will not give him my soul and you will not have me either. I will leave here and find my parents." They laughed again and showed their teeth. "It is not for you to decide boy and the master will either die or you will die." With that they turned and walked to the edge of the field. The stalker turned to him before disappearing and waved his hand in the air. A smell filled the air and Tristan turned to see his mother and father standing in the field staring at him. Tears welled in his eyes and he ran to them in disbelief. His parents went to their knees and wrapped their arms around him hugging so hard they thought they would hurt him. The creature walked into the shadows and left them for the master. Jody kissed his head and looked him over as she did when had gotten hurt. "Mom, Dad, where is the man?" Dustin looked towards the house. "You do not need to go back there, son. You need to run and forget about this place." Jody cried and held her boy close to her chest. The house smoked and churned in the distance. They knew he was there watching and waiting for their son to come home. He wouldn't take him in the fields where the others could see. He promised them that Tristan would give them salvation, and he would kill him in the house and then rid of him. Tristan looked at his parents and pulled away. "He will come and I need to go." All around them the shadows formed into silhouettes and the inhabitants of the field filled in around them. "He is right sir," the young black man said. "The master will come. We know what his plans are but this boy is different. He will not die like other boys before him." Dustin let him go and tears filled his eyes. Jody did the same and the silhouettes gathered around them. "You go now boy and see the master. You will lead us to salvation, he fears you. Be strong now." Tristan stepped away into the field and faced the house. The tree stood in the corner swaying back and forth like a giant protector. Its branches stretching into the field caressing it like children. He turned to watch the silhouettes fade and he blew a kiss to his mother and smiled. "I love you," he said quietly. He knew they loved him and he never needed to hear it. He stood in the darkness of the field alone, the wind calling his name as the grass tickling his calves. The house reminded him of his dad's movies and he realized that this was a bad time to recollect on scary movies. The smoke filled the air like a giant cape and he could hear its whispers telling him to stay away. The master waited for him and there was no choice. If he ran like his father had told him, he would never be far enough away. The master would find him and the others would suffer for it. He wondered what happened to John and thought that the master had probably killed himas he ran into the field. He heard John yell his name and never looked back to see what had happened.

He tried to think of a better situation for him but knew that he was not with us anymore. He began to walk slowly to the house and realized that it was a good two hundred yards. This gave him time to think of what he would do when he saw the master. How would he stop him from killing him and continuing on finding others? From the corner of his eye he saw the creature at the edge of the field. The others were not with him and he jetted in and out of view beside him. Its voice rang out into the field. "Do not hesitate boy, he fears you and knows you are not alone." Tristan did not understand what he was talking about and continued to walk towards the house, looking at the tree, as it swayed towards the field. He remembered his mother yelling his dad to get rid of that tree and wondered what his father's thoughts were now. The creature continued to follow him on the edge and chant clicks and clacks into the air. Tristan couldn't make out the noises this time and chose to focus on the house now only fifty yards away. He could make out the yard and looked around the property to see if the master was visible. He could hear the tree creek and bend to show its strength to the field. Tristan knew to stay away from it and enter from the center of the yard. The master knew he was here and trying to sneak in was just prolonging the confrontation. When he stepped into the yard the creature at his side stopped and clicked up at the tree in anger. The great beast ignored the creature and swayed heavy in Tristan's direction. It couldn't reach him and he stood his ground looking up at the smoking house. *Where are you?* The smell of the wood made his eyes sting and the yard would fill with smoke and then clear making him squint to see two feet in front of him. The master was inside and Tristan knew that going inside would be the end. If the master didn't consume him the smoke would. He glanced at the tree and watched as the creature jumped up at its branches and laughed as it swayed over it in anger. Suddenly, the creature turned and bolted deeper into the field. Tristan was shocked at how fast it moved and remembered that night in his room looking out into the field from his window. What made it bolt so quickly; "The boy returns", he heard from the porch. When he turned back to the house, the master stood on the porch and stared him down. The tree began to relax and the smoke seemed to clear the yard and avoid any contact with the porch or him. Tristan wasn't scared and stood there silent waiting to see what he would do. "Did you come to confront me son? I can't say I'm not impressed." He walked along the porch and looked out into the field. "Where did your little minion go?He could hear the creature far away and looked at the master and shrugged his shoulders. The master was surprised at how calm the boy was. Many before him had cried and screamed for mercy, the fact that this boy did not made him slightly nervous. It had never left his mind that this could be the one that led them away from his field, the savior, the one that held salvation. "Do you think you will save them from me, your mommy and daddy? The others are foolish you know." Tristan just stood quiet and watched him realizing that he was nervous. "Well," the master continued. "You are not the first to be chosen to see them through. There had been hundreds before you and not one Tristan has gotten through me, not one." "What is it that you are scared of?" Tristan spoke loudly. The master stopped in his tracks and stood surprised at the boy's manner. "You are sure of yourself." He said. "Did the shadow dwellers get you believing their banter? They look out for their master whom you would not want any part of I assure you." He paced the porch and crossed his arms studying the boy. "You know your friend Mr. Stathom? He died like a worm trying to make a deal with me. I really hope you do not go the same way Tristan" His fear factor wasn't working,this he realized as Tristan stood unaffected by his story. The master began to pace a little faster and then stopped and stared right into the boy's eyes. "You will come to me and die like a good little maggot. You will not destroy what is rightfully mine and you will spend the rest of your days eating your own feces with those creatures in the fields." He stepped down the steps to the yard. He stopped when Tristan stood still and showed no emotion. "If you kill me then I will be with my parents and the people in the field will see you here and they will abandon you." The master stopped and looked out into the field and could see the silhouettes appear at the yards border behind Tristan. He turned and looked to the tree that was now still and quiet. The inhabitants of the field stayed at the edge and remained nothing more but shadows as the master took another step into the yard. "He is not the chosen one!" He yelled. "He will not lead you to salvation." Tristan stood there and could feel the others behind him. The energy pulsed through his body and made him relax and become one with the field. The grass swayed in his direction and the great tree leaned towards him.

He closed his eyes and stood in the wind and could feel his soul above his body. The master stepped into the yard and advanced towards the boy. "He is nothing and you shall not defy me any longer!" Tristan leaned back, the master ran up to him and raising his fist, he plunged it straight into the child's chest and ripped his heart out taking some of his rib cage with it. He opened his mouth as the boy's body fell to the ground and devoured the organ, blood spilling all over his face and chest. The master laughed into the field as the silhouettes stepped back into the shadows. The tree shook and leaned away towards the yard as the wind cried. Smoke engulfed him and he summoned it away with a wave of his hand. When the smoke cleared he could see Tristan standing at the field's edge. The inhabitants stood beside him and stared at the master silent and still. "Did you think the boy would save you and take you from my field?" They didn't answer and looked as the tree became still the wind stopping. He dropped the remainder of the organ in the yard and walked to the field's edge and looked down at the boy. "He was nothing but a sign to you, that's all." The blood from his body was pulled into the field by the grass and the inhabitants looked up at the master. The young black man stepped forward, "It was you who thought he was just a sign. We have already understood his meaning, you are blind." The master wiped his mouth with his fist and gave a wide smirk. "The ferry man will not come for any of you and you will all remain here, in the fields until I decide salvation." His eyes were like fire and the fog around his body hovered over him like a cloak. "You have already decided long ago," the young man looked out beyond the field and the inhabitants parted,there in the field stood Tristan, his little body surrounded by fog. "As you can see, salvation is here." The master looked out, without hesitation, leapt into the field withhuge strides straight for Tristan. The boy did not move and just stared. Out from the edge of the field the three demons cut through the grass and made their way into outer shadows to watch. They clucked and chirped, their eyes danced in the grass as the master picked up speed. As he approached, Tristan held out both of his arms and everything stopped, air, the grass, and time. The eyes stopped dancing and the smoke from the house sat in the sky like watercolors. Tristan's palms faced the sky, in them sat two shiny quarters. Everything was quite. He listened for a moment and shut his eyes. It was peaceful, and for the first time in a long time, he felt at home. All the seizures, doctors, boring days and sleepless nights, all the times he wondered if he would ever be normal again like other childrenhad just vanished. He was home, his field now. He looked over at the demons, smiles pasted across their face in laughter. He couldn't think of them like that and it made him smile to think that for a brief moment they were more than just keepers of the field. As he looked past the master and toward the house a figure began to emerge from the still smoke. He had suddenly wonderedwhere his mother and father were and if they had already made out of the field? As the figure approached Tristan could see that it was wearing a robe. Without further thought he knew it was the ferry man. A voice boomed out from under the hood and pulled back Tristan's cheeks making his face taunt. The voice was a low octave that bellowed through the field, reminding him of elephants at the zoo when he was a little boy. The sound laid the grass flat and shook the horizon and he thought it might be the devil himself as the voice cracked and snapped, "You are the chosen that the inhabitants have spoken of, yes?" The master's clothes flapped about as the monstrous voice drummed on. The noise abruptly stopped and Tristan took a deep breath in. Without another sound the figure walked up to Tristan and removed his hood. His face was young, maybe twenty, Tristan was surprised at how warm and peaceful he looked. The young man smiled and looked around the field as if there was something he was looking for. "You are the ferry man right?" The man looked back at Tristan and smiled, "Yes." He walked over to the master and looked up at him. "Mmmm, this one I remember," he looked back at Tristan slightly bent, "the master of the field."He paused and returned to his study. He flipped his arm up and down slowly, "Lower your hands boy." Tristan put his arms down to his sides, clenching the coins. "Is that payment?" he smiled as he looked at Tristan's fists. Tristan looked down at the quarters and then held one out. The man ignored him and continued to look around the hovering menace. "When he had first came to the field,s he refused to acknowledge he was dead," he stopped and turned back to Tristan. "It took only a few years here for him to realize that he would never leave." He walked around Tristan and glanced over at the frozen demons, not giving too much time for attention. "Why was he here for so long without knowing?" "He knew, and it was a shame that he couldn't go to the other side. He came to me with the others." Tristan looked up at the master and back to the ground thinking. "Well," he continued. "When they all came to me, payment was rendered, except Mr. Peters. He had no living relatives that came here, well not to stay." He looked over to the demons again. The ferry man shrugged his shoulders and returned the conversation to the boy. "And so, Mr. Peters stayed here, year after year. It's been more than one hundred years." Tristan walked up to the master and studied his stone stare. "His name was Mr. Peters?" The ferry man smiled, "Yes. He used to own the farm house and the slaves that dwelled there." He began to wander in circles and talk to himself more than Tristan. "I could never understand man's desire to hurt each other in such a fashion. It's shame what happened to those people there." The man looked out to the horizon, the sky was lightening and the shadows slowly began to retreat. Within a few hours it would be dawn and a new day for the fields. The ferry man never spent much time in the fields during the dawn and it was something he took in when it occurred. "Why can he never leave the fields, he must have someone on the other side to go to." "No," the man turned. "What he did to those people is hell's work and that's where he should be" he said. Tristan walked over to the man and stared out to the horizon. "Why is it in the fields then?" "He made a deal with those, maggots," he looked out the corner of his eye towards demons. "He stays if they stay." Tristan put it all together and looked down at his coins. "What do we do now?" The man pulled his hood back over his head and began to walk out into the field without saying a word. Tristan turned towards the master and he felt a breeze blow past his face as everything animated to life again. The master flew through the air and landed in a patch and was startled that he hadn't landed on the boy. The demons clinked and clicked behind Tristan as the master looked up and stared right into Tristan's eyes. "Were you going boy, you think your mother and father can help you, maybe those beasts over there, huh? He sneered at the demons. They returned the glare and walked out a little further. Tristan understood the pecking order now and could tell they were waiting for him to take the master down so they could drag him to hell were he belonged. The master stood tall and his mouth slowly spread open showing his twisted teeth, his tongue slithering out and licking his chin. "You need to realize that you can't escape me boy and just make it clear what position you are in," he snapped his finger and Tristan's parent appeared floating next to the master. Their flesh was gray and twisted and their eyes were white and glossed over. "This is what they have in store if you don't get over here and face your destiny." Tristan stared at his parents and tears filled his eyes and poured down his cheeks. He could feel anger building in him and he stared down Mr. Peters and for the first time in his life felt pure hate. "It will be you that perishes here in the field Mr. Peters." He snapped. The master's eyes flashed fire and he clapped his hands letting the bodies of Judy and Dustin fall to the grass like pieces of useless meat. "Who told you my name boy, how dare you use it here in my fields." Tristan let a small smile cross his lips and with that he held up one of his quarters. "You see this Mr. Peters, remember what this stands for?" The master glared at the coin, the fire rose in his eyes brighter, his tongue slashed at the air as he began to breath heavy. "This is something you weren't privileged with when you went to the ferry man was it?" The master lifted his arms in the air and let out a screech that toppled the grass and shook the ground. Tristan covered his ears and dropped the coin to the ground. The master shook with anger and the fire in his eyes burst out from the sockets as his tongue licked the flames turning the tip black. The demons in the distance watched with excitement, pacing back and forth while they clucked at each other and scrapped the ground. The shadows receded almost back to the edge of the field now and the sun began to climb the horizon like a phoenix. Tristan knew that the master feared the demons and him more. It was an act to keep the others under his control and it began to fall apart by the second. One at a time, the inhabitants of the field began to appear and the master looked around screeching louder and louder. Tristan thought his head would explode as he watched the field begin to fill with shadows. One at a time they formed around them and the master began to settle down. He looked around and focused on them as Tristan regained posture. He shot a stare back at Tristan and began to walk over to him, raising his fist and bearing his teeth. His tongue continued to slash at the air, wrapping around the back of his head like a serpent. Tristan stood his ground and gnashed his teeth and was ready. When Mr. Peters got with swinging distance a figure formed between the boy and him that made him pull back quick and back up a few feet. The ferry man stood there and stared at him with no emotion. "What is it you planned to do here Mr. Peters?" The master bent and grimaced at the man, "Take care of unfinished business that doesn't need to worry you good sir." The man looked around at the inhabitants and raised his hand in the air. "You must all come with me, it is your time for salvation my friends, you have overstayed your welcome here in the fields." The inhabitants began to walk foreword and past Mr. Peters. He retaliated with snarls but did nothing more knowing that the ferry man controlled these fields. "I'll come for you all. You will not pass into salvation!"As they continued to walk into the field, Tristan looked on confused and amazed. *Why was I needed, why did my family suffer?* "Because you were the one to get them to follow and all great leaders suffer." The ferry man said. Tristan watched as the inhabitants emptied the field. When the last had past he looked at the master and saw the fear in his eyes. "You have done this to yourself Mr. Peters. You should have never stayed in the fields." The demons crept closer licking their lips and realizing that the time was at hand. They would bring the bastard home and they didn't care if they could never return to the fields. The hatred and blood from the master was century's payment. The field was now empty and they would go home until it filled again. The master began to panic and he let out screeches as he watched them fade into the horizon. The ferry man turned ignoring the master and Tristan, joining the others heading towards the horizon. Jody and Dustin rose from the ground and walked past Tristan brushing their hands across his shoulder. "Come son," Dustin smiled. "We have people on the other side that await us." Tristan looked at the master, turned and began to walk away. The demons approached slowly and stopped looking at the empty field. "So Mr. Peters, shall we close the deal. I do believe your end of our bargain had expired and you have family waiting as well." The master backed up a little and turned to the house. The smoke began to clear as the sun blasted the side of the house to life. The tree stood quietly as its leaves turned to catch the rays. The field was bright green and alive leaving Peters with the realization that his stay was at its end. He didn't hesitate as he sprinted for the house. The demons hissed and took after him grabbing tusks of grass as they snarled. The front man let out a war call that made Peters panic and almost loose his footing. He looked over his shoulder and caught the glimpse of the three ripping through the field after him. When he reached the yard he darted from the side of the house. The farther he got from the field meant they would have to give up chase. They were not permitted too far from the field. Either was he but he would rather burst into flames and burn there in sun then in hell. As he got close to the side of the yard he took one more look back and saw that they were standing at the fields edge smiling. He stood there and began to laugh and pointed at them. They would not get him today. "I'll see you hell my friends!" he yelled. When he turned around he froze as the tree bent down its arms reached out grabbing Peters and raising him high above the ground. The demons danced and raised their hands in the air as they watched the tree swing their prey back and forth. Screams filled the air and blood began to pour down like rain as his body was torn in two and flung overhead. Twistinglike witches, they went into the fields and danced as the blood rained down upon them,opening their mouths and drinking till they were full. The tree slowed down and swayed calmly back and forth as the sun made the red on the shine. The bottom torso of the former master hung in the branches and the upper half was deeper in the tree. He was still alive and the tree groaned and pulled him out of its nest and raised him as high as the branches could reach. At the edge of the horizon the ferry man stopped and looked back towards the house. He could barely make out the commotion of the demons dancing, but knew that Mr. Peters would have his last days on the surface of this planet. Tristan walked with his parents and hugged his dad's waist. The field ended and before them there was now a great darkness. All of the inhabitants stood and waited. None of them understood what would happen and what salvation would bring them. From the darkness emerged a huge boat. As it approached, light from its bow revealed a glistening sea underneath it. The water was like silver with a deep purple just under its waves. They all stepped back as the ferry man walked past them and raised his hands. "This is your salvation, come with me and I shall bring you to your destiny." Tristan stepped forward and looked at the man. "What am I to pay, I was the one. I have no coins." The ferry man walked up to him and bent down to him. "There was no coins my boy, you are here and that was the payment. You are the chosen one and have brought them away from Mr. Peters. You are the payment." Tristan smiled and his mother put her arm around his shoulder and squeezed him. "We all shall be together forever," she said quietly. They all began to load onto the boat and from the back stepped the young black man. He looked at Tristan and nodded to Dustin and Jody. "See," he smiled. "He's a strong child and he was to lead us to salvation. Just believe Mr. Burns." Dustin nodded and watched as he passed and joined the others in the line. When all the inhabitants were upon the boat Dustin, Jody and Tristan climbed aboard and disappeared into the darkness, into salvation. The demons back in the fields looked up at the tree and beckoned it to release their winnings. It was as if it wanted to relish in its feat, its new freedom. The master was no more and it could wither and die and return to the earth to be born anew. With a huge sway the tree bent back and then flung foreword and slammed the two halves of the master to the ground, digging up dirt and grass. The demons jumped back and were almost taken out by the trees mighty branches. They cheered and jumped as it swung back and left the remains for them in the field. They scrambled over to him and bounced around the pieces in frenzy. The group leader looked up to the horizon and then grabbed one of the legs as one of the other beasts grabbed the other. They tore it like a wishbone, the leader getting the bigger half. The other clucked and bit the air in disappointment with his take. The upper half of the torso was left for the third and he began to drag it deeper into the field to the shadows of the wooded edge. They chanted and tossed pieces of organs and limbs that fell free into the air and left them to the field for the animals to feed. The house stood quietly and the last puff of smoke bellowed into the sky. The backdoor way that led into the house told the story of what transpired the night before. The family that lived here would nothing more than a story and the fields will rest for a time. The demons' chanting faded as they crept into the distance and took the once feared master with them home. The grass rippled and whispered as the wind blew it back and forth. The field was once more nothing more than a field. The sun climbed to mid sky and beamed down upon the farm. John's car sat abandoned just off the side of the road crows began to feed on Brunnel and Kent's remains. A car rumbled past the broken cell phone in the road and sped past the house. The dust from the road swirled into the air and faded as the sound of the driver's radio filled the air and passed over the field.

CHAPTER 13

For the last thirty days the temperature stayed relatively the same, the only thing that really felt any different than home was the locals and the food. The tables reminded him of his grandmother's swimming pool furniture and he looked up at the umbrella over head and felt the sun burn through to his face. Casa Del Mar was as nice as it was going to get, and for the time being and he wasn't complaining. Jacuzzis and pretty girls with golden skin floated around the pool and smiled casually, practically making him order them a drink. It had been five months since he had been in Mexico and not one day had past when he didn't think of Brunnel, Kent, and the kid. Nights were always interrupted when he woke up in a sweat. He couldn't get the vision of the bodies laying in the grass and the animals ripping at their bodies. A waitress stopped as he stared at the table. "Would you like another drink sir?" Mitchelle looked up and smiled, coming out of his trance. She was young and beautiful and again he just shook his head, "Yes that would be wonderful." As she walked away he thought about what a sucker he was and if he didn't work on that soon he would go broke. He grabbed the newspaper off the table and leaned back in his chair. He would have to find work soon id he was going to stay in the clean business. It amazed him how hard it was to find work and could now fully sympathize with the unemployed. She returned with his drink and placed on the table giving him that sexy smile again. He pulled out a five dollar bill from his shorts and handed it to her reluctantly, *gotta work on that.* A couple of young kids walked by and he watched as they pushed each other and laughed about whatever the joke of the hour was. He could stay here forever and it dropped his mood when he thought about how that was not a reality. He liked the European resorts better and wished he had the funds to hop a plane to Paris or maybe Italy. Again that was another dream he would need to put aside. The real world situation was closing in on him and he knew that getting a real job meant uncontrolled bills and the like. No more wine and dine in Vegas or hopping that plane to Romania for some odd ball job that would only further the spiral into descent. The only thing he knew was employment of the illegal persuasion and it was apparent to him that the "straight job" was going to be challenging and nothing he was looking forward to. He thumbed through the help wanted ads and grunted at the numerous restaurant and construction jobs that barked benefit packages and thirty an hour wages. Thirty dollars an hour wouldn't have gotten anything done in his former employment *gotta work on that too.* He folded the paper and flopped on the table then finished his drink. Taking a walk had crossed his mind and so hadn't taking a dip in the pool but he was too lazy to bother with either one. The spot in which he sat seemed the best choice for now and he watched the beauties stroll by and took a break from that once in awhile to enjoy the laughter of the children that ran past. *Maybe the hotel was hiring?* That made him chuckle and he could picture himself with a little server suit on, "Would you like a drink?" He was losing his goddamn mind and he put his head in his hands to laugh for a second. The waitress returned and she stood there waiting for him to look up. Before she could even bat the smile he grinned, "No thank you, I do not need another drink at the moment." She just smiled and walked away to another table to prey on some other vacationer. He sat back in his chair and realized that the only thing he needed right now was a nice nap. He looked at his watch and scoffed at the time, one thirty in the afternoon. Feeling like an old man he stood up and fixed his shorts and took one last look around at the beautiful ladies hoping that he would see one in less attire as he slept. He walked across the grounds to the lobby and felt the blast of air condition hit his face. At the moment it felt good but knew that if he stayed any more than five minutes he would be freezing and have to step outside. Walking up to the receptionist he nodded his daily greeting, "any calls today?" She looked at her counter and then smiled up at him with gorgeous brown eyes. "No sir." She answered and he walked away with utter confusion as to how they seemed to manage to hire only gorgeous women at this place? *The world may never know.* The lobby was full of locals and vacationers looking in gift shops and ranting about the different tours they had been on throughout their stay. It was funny to him that they were oblivious to the fact that walking right past them was a man wanted in two countries and ten states in America. They were too busy buying tacky postcards to send to coworkers and uncaring family members. He made sure to enter the elevator as quickly as he could and get to the quietness of his room. Of course the elevator was the haven of all strangers and the most uncomfortable place known to man. He entered and looked only once at the man and women dressed in the standard vacationer attire, shorts and hotel embroidered t-shirt. He couldn't help but think of himself once again wearing the uniform and escorting people like this to their rooms. He didn't chuckle as much this time. He pushed the second floor button and the doors closed and he stared at them waiting and hoping that neither person struck up conversation. No such luck, "how long ya been here?" the man piped in. Mitchelle turned a little and smiled, "A week, and you?" The woman smiled and looked at the man, "Long enough to watch you Mitchelle." He spun around to the girl and both of them drew pistols. He was confused and tried to think of who they were. "Were did you hide the family?" she continued. Mitchelle heard the bell chime and then the doors opened to the second door hallway. The two put there pistols away as several people looked to get on. Mitchelle and the two entered the hallway and smiled as the others climbed in and the door shut. They could hear them chatting away as the elevator descended. Mitchelle knew better than to run so he stood there and stared at them. The man gave him a harsh look, "We went to the house and the family was nowhere to be seen, the local police even put out a search party for the bodies. They scoured that field for three days, nothing." Mitchelle shrugged his shoulders. "As soon as we get the child you are free to go," The woman said. "We found the bodies of your two buddies as well, don't worry we got rid of the chewed up corpses long before the local authorities arrived, lucky for you." "Why is that lucky for me," Mitchelle smirked, "The cops have no idea who I am." The man frowned at him and pulled his pistol. "Well," he smiled. "We made sure to report someone with your very well known description in the area at the time the family was reported missing, so we did ya a favor." He was led to his room and when he pulled his card to unlock the door he paused for a second. He thought of a thousand ways to get out of this situation and none of them seemed promising. When the door shut Mitchelle walked over to the window and sat at the little round table with the remnants of his breakfast. "I have no idea where they are, I left the scene without even going to the house." The two split up, the man walked over buy the closet and stayed closest to the door, the woman walked over next to the bed, "This isn't really time for bullshit Mitchelle, if you really do not have the kid then just tell us and we will be on our way." He looked at the woman and held his hands up and sat down. Slapping them down on his lap he shook his head, "I have no idea." She raised her left arm and fired three shots into his face. The silencer's puff echoed through the room as his body flopped against the back of the chair and he toppled to the floor. Blood splattered the window and the man walked up and grabbed a napkin from the breakfast tray, "Ahh," he complained, and wiped it up throwing it on the table when he was done. They looked once at Mitchelle and then walked out of the room and shut the door. Vacationers past them in the hall way and they smiled at one another as they entered the elevator. "What do you think happened to the kid?" She looked at him and shook her head. They would need to go back to the farm and hope that the police had left something or just overlooked important information. The room was quiet and the sounds of playing children muffled through the glass window were the only audible sounds. The smell of stale toast, cold eggs and blood filled the room as the heat beat through the widow intensifying the aroma. Mitchelle lay there staring at the wall across the room. The day everyone died at the field marked the last for Mitchelle. It could have gone without incident but the wind was just right.